WHO IS THE EXECUTIONER?

Meet Mack Bolan, combat hero of Korea and Viet Nam and now a one-man army fighting America's most insidious enemy – the Mafia.

In Viet Nam the military ledgers credit Bolan with more than 90 VC 'Kills'. He was an extraordinary soldier – and a man who worked at his job.

Then he returned home one summer to find his father, mother and sister dead. He traced the crime to a Mafia loan-shark's dealing with his father. That was the beginning of a new direction in Mack Bolan's war career.

'It looks like I have been fighting the wrong enemy,' he said. 'Why defend a front line 8,000 miles away when the real enemy is chewing up everything you love back home?'

Also by Don Pendleton

THE EXECUTIONER: MIAMI MASSACRE
THE EXECUTIONER: ASSAULT ON SOHO
THE EXECUTIONER: CHICAGO WIPEOUT
THE EXECUTIONER: VEGAS VENDETTA
THE EXECUTIONER: CARIBBEAN KILL

and published by Corgi Books

Don Pendleton

The Executioner:
Nightmare in New York

CORGI BOOKS
A DIVISION OF TRANSWORLD PUBLISHERS LTD

THE EXECUTIONER:
NIGHTMARE IN NEW YORK

A CORGI BOOK 0 552 09206 1

First publication in Great Britain

PRINTING HISTORY
Corgi edition published 1973
Corgi edition reprinted 1973

Copyright © 1971 by Pinnacle Books

This book is set 10 on 11 pt. Baskerville

Corgi Books are published by
Transworld Publishers Ltd.,
Cavendish House, 57–59 Uxbridge Road,
Ealing, London W.5.

Made and printed in Great Britain by
Cox & Wyman Ltd., London, Reading and Fakenham

Dedication

For Colonel Edward St. George, who must be Bolan's oldest living friend. Here's to you, St. George, and to a most vigorous and active 94th year of life.
Kilauea!

PROLOGUE

SOME have said that Mack Bolan was a genius in the tactics and strategies of guerilla warfare. He has been called a death machine, a blitz artist, a one-man army. Newspaper headlines have referred to him as the monster man, the grinder, the awesome avenger, the Mafia nightmare. Whatever the tag, all agreed that Bolan was an executioner without equal; that in this single man stood the greatest challenge ever hurled upon the spreading menace of the Mafia kingdoms of America.

As is inevitable in cases which catch the public fancy, a great mass of legend arose around the man – some of it true, much of it not so true. Bolan was not, for example, being sponsored by the U.S. Justice Department or the CIA. He did not have a license to kill. Local police agencies were not following him about to pounce on his victims when he was done with them. He did not accumulate a fortune by plundering his enemies' money caches nor did he, à la Robin Hood, redistribute the Mafia's wealth. He did not perform ceremonial executions, he did not possess a dozen faces, he had not sworn to kill every criminal in the country, and he did not have the protection of a special Secret Service detail.

The truth about Bolan's campaign against the Mafia is not quite so sensationally romantic as the legend; typically, however, the truth is much more chillingly awesome than the fiction. The facts are that Bolan was a man alone pitted against the most staggering array of enemies ever faced by a single man, and that he waged this impossible war without sponsorship or direct support from any quarter. It is true that a highly placed official in the Justice Department did approve of Bolan's war and was discreetly maneuvering behind the scenes to ease federal pressures toward his apprehension. It is true that Bolan knew the identity of an undercover cop who had achieved high rank in a Mafia family, and that these two did occasionally enjoy friendly relations and an intelligence trade-off. It is true that some policemen did 'look the other way' when Bolan was about, recognizing in him not an enemy but a true ally who would accept death rather than engage the law in a shootout.

It is equally factual, however, that a concerted drive was underway at every level of law enforcement to apprehend Mack Bolan dead or alive. It is factual that a death contract had been let on Bolan by the Mafia and that bands of ambitious bounty-hunters from every section of the country were determined to collect the $100,000 payoff on that contract. And it is, of course, common knowledge that Bolan was hated and feared by every *Mafioso* everywhere, so that the full power of the sprawling crime syndicate was committed to the destruction of this lone warrior who challenged their might with such impunity.

Genius, death machine, blitz artist, one-man army – yes, it is true that, in his effect, Bolan was all of these. At the heart of this man, though, lay a sensitive and uncomplicated human being who had simply recognized and accepted the challenge placed upon his manhood. He did not see himself as an heroic figure; he knew well that heroes are usually quite ordinary men who find themselves thrust suddenly into heroic situations. He did not view his actions as a holy crusade which was self-justified; quite often his self-doubts were immense and his revulsion to killing almost overpowering. He did not gladly sacrifice the earlier plan of his life to this gory walk through the valley of death; like most men he had desired for himself the simple things that give life meaning – what Bolan termed 'the three F's of the good life: friends, family, freedom'. Reluctantly he had surrendered this quiet ambition to the three B's – 'bullets, bombs, and blood'.

And yet Bolan's incredible war had not begun with such conscious volition. He had been engaged in a quite different battle, though a conflict considered by some to be just as immoral as Bolan's personal one. It was in Vietnam that he developed the guerilla specialties which earned the young sergeant local fame as *The Executioner*. As leader and sharp-shooter of a special penetration team, Bolan had 'executed' numerous enemy officials and high ranking enemy officers often spending extended periods deep within enemy country. Then one of those everyday and little-heard-of brutalities of American life resulted in Sergeant Bolan being called home to bury his father, his mother, and his younger sister. Sam Bolan, an ailing steelworker, had found himself caught in the vicious squeeze of a Mafia loan sharking operation. Though he had repaid the principal several times over on a grossly usurious loan, the elder Bolan had been terrorized, beaten and hounded to the limits of human endurance by brutal collectors. Learning, then, that his teen-age-daughter had been pressured into prostitution to help retire the loan, Sam Bolan had crossed that line of human endurance, had gone berserk, and had killed his daughter, his wife, and himself. These were the circumstances of Sergeant Bolan's homecoming. Only young Johnny Bolan, the kid brother, survived to provide the details behind the triple-tragedy.

When the grieving soldier discovered that there was no recourse to justice under the law, he took justice unto himself and *The Executioner* shifted his battle zone to the home front. He penetrated the inner family, found the men responsible for Sam Bolan's misery, and he executed them. As an act of personal justice and vengeance fulfilled, this should have ended things. It did not. A police official in his home town of Pittsfield offered to write off this initial campaign as a gang war if Bolan would just go back to the army and never return. Bolan could not do so. He had become too familiar with the enemy, he knew their evil, and he could

9

not turn his back on this creeping menace that promised to smother all that was good and decent – all that Bolan had felt he had been fighting for in Vietnam. The greater enemy was *here*, at home, not in a backward little country eight thousand miles away.

Bolan remained to engage that greater enemy, and the Bolan wars were begun. In a thunder and lightning brand of warfare which was to become his trademark, he smashed the Mafia arm which had dominated his home town, and the war without end and without geographical boundaries was loudly proclaimed by *Mafiosi* everywhere.

Following the hit and fade strategy of the guerilla jungle fighter, Bolan transformed the wide world into a jungle of his own making, surfacing here and there for a lightning assault that left the enemy shaken and benumbed, then fading again with all the hounds of hell baying along his trail through the closing jungle.

The story which follows is the seventh chronicle of the Bolan wars. The first two reports covered his destruction of the Sergio Frenchi Family of Pittsfield and the first encounter with the DiGeorge Family of Southern California. The third report saw Bolan with a new face, thanks to plastic surgery, and a devastating infiltration of the DiGeorge Family which left that kingdom a shambles. Number four reported Bolan's uninvited participation in the Mafia's national convention at Miami Beach in a daring raid that violently rocked the Mafia ship of state and showed the collective families of *La Cosa Nostra* that Mack Bolan was a force to be reckoned with.

The fifth and sixth segments found Bolan unwillingly overseas and hotly pursued by pyramiding crews of Mafia headhunters through France and England. During the peripheral actions of these two adventures, he has begun to come into a deeper understanding of the true significance of his war with syndicated evil. In this seventh campaign, the realization is strongly upon Bolan that he has been waging a futile brand of warfare. The mob is indeed ever-present, all-knowing, and very nearly all-powerful. A war of attrition can have no meaning here. By sheer weight of numbers he is doomed to lose this war, and the final balance sheet will reflect no measurable impact upon the enemy.

In Bolan's own understanding, then, Phase Two of his Mafia War has ended, Phase Three is beginning. The War of Attrition is giving way to the War of Destruction. He will hit them now in their omniscience; in their omnipotence; their omnipresence, he reasons, will then fold under its own weight.

Bolan is in the saddle, his mount is destiny, his target is the *Kingdom of Evil* – wherever its ugly head may arise.

FACES

FOUR faces of death awaited him as he stepped into the main terminal area at Kennedy International. Bolan went on without a pause but his mental mug-file clicked to a halt at a quick make on Sam 'The Bomber' Chianti, a contract specialist in the Manhattan-based Gambella Family. The other three faces had no identity beyond the screamingly obvious imprint of Mafia street soldiers.

Bolan casually transferred the topcoat to his right arm, allowing it to cover the hand. His eyes, behind the dark glasses, swept on beyond the four hardmen as he moved smoothly past them and into the flow of traffic toward the helicopter station of Manhattan Airways. They had made him, of course — tagging along behind now, unbunching and fanning out like wranglers on a roundup.

Sam the Bomber was on Bolan's right flank. The other faces, glimpsed briefly yet seared now into his mental file, were keeping a discreet distance and covering any possible angle of escape, efficiently criss-crossing in the crowd, maintaining the rear seal.

A man ahead of Bolan was complaining loudly to a companion about the high cost of fun at Frankfurt. Bolan himself was thinking tiredly about the high cost of coming home and confronting the enemy unarmed. He had felt it wise to abandon his hardware at London Airport rather than risk detection by the hi-jack-conscious air marshals. The gamble had been for a quiet re-entry into the U.S. Bolan should have known better. Now he did. Too late.

With death stalking him, the survival instincts of the professional combat man took over and began directing Bolan. Sam the Bomber was moving in, quickly closing the gap between them. Bolan spoke without turning his head or breaking pace. 'You ready to die, Sam?' he asked coldly.

'Huh?' the other man grunted, caught offguard by the direct remark and briefly uncoordinated, his hand jerking toward the opening in his coat.

Bolan held the fast pace and snapped a glance at the dumbfounded hood. 'It's a setup,' he growled, his face unconcerned but his guts churning. 'Feds are all over me. You too, now.'

'Bullshit,' Chianti replied, vocally rejecting the warning. His eyes, however, were not all that positive, sliding about in an involuntary inspection of the crowd.

'So you'll be buried in bullshit. It's your last contract, Sam.' Bolan was rounding the corner to the helicopter station. The flustered Chianti moved a step too close going into the turn. Bolan's arm moved in a sudden blur, the topcoat whipped across the *Mafioso's* face, and Bolan's elbow slammed into his gut.

Chianti's breath left him with a whooshing gurgle. A short-barreled .38 revolver which had momentarily occupied his gun hand disappeared as suddenly as it had arrived and dropped into Bolan's waiting pocket as though the transfer had been a carefully rehearsed one. Bolan's hammering forearm chopped into the hardman's throat. He staggered back into the fast moving stream of traffic, going to the floor and taking several pedestrians down with him.

Bolan went on, leaving the confusion behind and merging with the main swirl through the gates. He snapped a backward glance as he crowded into the waiting helicopter and quickly located two anxious faces in the pileup at the boarding gate. The doors closed behind him and Bolan found a seat. Moments later the big ferry craft was lifting into the air. Through the window Bolan saw Sam the Bomber, his face a study in rage and frustration as he stepped into a phone booth.

Bolan sighed and fingered Chianti's .38 through the fabric of his jacket. So now it would be a race with time. The chopper would be putting down in midtown Manhattan in a matter of minutes. And another head party would be scrambling to get there ahead of him.

Bolan tried to relax, knowing that he could not. He scowled darkly at his reflection in the window. A guy did not go to his own execution all sweetly composed and ready for a gentle sigh into that last breath of life. Not this guy. His last breath would be a snarl, not a sigh.

The Midtown Station was perched atop a skyscraper not far from Grand Central Station. The ungainly craft settled onto the rooftop landing pad and Bolan was the first passenger to the door. He showed the crew man his pistol and told him, 'Go ahead and open up, but don't let anyone out for one full minute. There might be some gun play when I hit that roof. Understand?'

The crew man's face paled. He nodded his head in understanding.

Bolan asked him. 'Is the escape hatch forward, same as on the military version?'

Again the crew man nodded.

'Okay. Remember, one full minute.' Bolan found the emergency exit in the copter floor, opened it, and quickly dropped to the roof of the building. The rotors were still chugging overhead as he swung out beneath the belly and ran for the steps to the elevator area.

In the periphery of his vision, Bolan saw a large man with both arms extended step from behind a bricked area directly opposite the landing pad, and at the same moment a heavy-calibre handgun began to fire. Whistling slugs tore across Bolan's path and plowed into a ventilator housing just beyond. The guy was targeting on him from a firing-range stand, one hand grasping and steadying the gun wrist as he continued to coolly squeeze off round after round.

Bolan snap-fired two running shots from the .38 – both missing, but close enough to send the gunman scurrying for cover. A confusion of shouted commands and the sounds of running feet accompanied Bolan to the stairway which led to the raised deck, where a little guy with a big gun appeared at the top just as Bolan was starting up. The man at the top tried to dodge but Bolan's instinctive trigger finger had already dispatched an untidy hole directly between the retreating eyes. The gun went over the railing as the small man flopped onto the stairway. Bolan stepped aside to be clear of the falling body, then raced on to the top as a thick voice from below called up to him. 'You ain't got a chance, Bolan! We got you sealed on this roof!'

Bolan did not doubt the truth of that for a moment. But he had three seal dissolvers left in the revolver and he meant to spend them wisely. He sprinted across the raised area, then launched himself into a rolling dive as an assortment of handguns began unloading on him from the elevator shelter. He took a searing hit in the meaty part of his left shoulder then another burned across the flesh of his hip. Firing from the prone, Bolan squeezed off three deliberate shots into the crouching figures at the elevator, toppling them like dummies in a shooting gallery. Then he sneered away the pain alarms from the shrieking shoulder and lurched to his feet for an eyes-on confrontation with the final remaining obstacle to freedom. The guy was bent forward at the waist, a big auto-loader thrust out in front of him, and he was wildly jerking the trigger against an empty or jammed magazine, slowly backing into the elevator car.

Bolan transferred the now useless .38 to the equally useless and dangling left hand and sent a mental command to the damaged limb to hang on for just another moment, and he went in after the quickly dissolving seal. The guy saw death coming for him and his eyes began to roll. The automatic clattered to the floor and the hood's hands went to the back of his head. He croaked, 'Jeez, Bolan, I—'

Bolan's good right hand shot out to grab the guy's tie, and he catapulted him out of there in an arcing swing from the throat just as another group charged to the top of the stairway from the helicopter area. The guy was dancing around just outside the elevator, trying to keep his footing against the wild eviction fling. Guns thundered from the stairway and the *Mafioso*'s dancing took on a freakish quality as he stopped the hot missiles meant for Bolan. The elevator doors, closing, also intercepted a grouping of sizzling metal. Then the car was in motion and Bolan was alone with his empty revolver and a steadily building pain in his shoulder. The pistol slipped away from numbed fingers and his lifeblood followed closely, dropping into bright scarlet spots on the floor. He wadded a handkerchief and jammed it roughly inside his shirt, holding it tightly and grinding his teeth against the new onslaught of harsh sensation.

The firefight on the roof had seemed to last an eternity. Actually, hardly more than a minute had elapsed since he dropped from the belly of that chopper. Men died in a fingersnap; time seemed to stand still at moments like that. It was not standing still now. Bolan's shoulder wound was bleeding furiously, and he could literally *feel* the life energies seeping away from him. He had not escaped, he knew – only delayed the end a while longer.

The elevator was an automatic express between the roof and the thirty-eighth floor. He left it at that level and took another car to the sixteenth floor, then doubled back to the twentieth. There he carefully cleaned up some wet splotches of spilled blood and went looking for the stairway, taking care not to leave a telltale trail of crimson.

The arm was beginning to stiffen, his coatsleeve was soaked, and the bleeding was showing no signs of letting up. The grazed hip was stinging like hell but had bled very little and was obviously not going to give him much trouble. Not that he needed any more. Those guys on the roof would not be giving up all that easy. At that moment, Bolan knew, they were swarming the building in a determined effort to keep him sealed in there. And, of course, in a minute or two there would be cops to contend with. There would always be cops, as dependable as heat in hell.

The shoulder was not hurting much now. That was a bad sign. Also his legs were getting rubbery and his eyes were becoming unreliable. The truth bore in on his dizzied consciousness – he would not find that stairway, and it would not do him much good if he should. He was losing consciousness. He stumbled, and threw his good hand out to steady himself against the wall. Instead he fell against the frosted glass of a door and his hand came to rest on the doorknob. Artful letters on the door told him that *Paul's Fashions* lay just inside.

Bolan pushed on inside just as his legs gave way altogether and the floor of the office floated up to receive him. A feminine voice squealed something in an alarmed falsetto, and impossibly long and shapely legs ran over to stand beside him. Then a pretty face was hovering above his and a disembodied voice gasped, 'Oh wow! I know who you . . .'

Bolan had lost his dark glasses somewhere back there in the fracas. Sure, everyone knew who he was. That face of his had been plastered across newspapers, national magazines, and television screens so often that it had become almost as familiar to the American public as John Wayne's or Paul Newman's.

His voice sounded to him as though it were coming from soneone else as he feebly commanded, 'Call the cops and leave!' Death crews left no witnesses, and suddenly the most important thing in his spinning mind was to warn this girl of her danger. 'Quick, get out before . . .' The words became entangled in his tongue and he lost them.

Another pair of legs floated in from somewhere. The same

voice he'd heard before was declaring, 'It's that guy, that Executioner.'

'Some executioner,' said another, less excited, female. 'It looks as though he tried once too often.'

With his final erg of conscious energy, Bolan whispered, 'Don't get caught here with me. Run, *now – split*!'

Then the most incredibly beautiful face he had ever seen was hanging there just above his, inspecting him with a concerned smile, and he took that image with him into the beckoning whirlpool of utter blackness. Perhaps, he thought, he would not die with a snarl, after all. If he was dying, then it was with a quiet sigh of deepest regret.

BODIES

Bolan dreamed of lush Elysian Fields and of cavorting with beautiful naked nymphs with impossibly long legs, and of skinny-dipping in sparkling pools where the nymphs grew Mafia heads beneath their arms. The dream seemed uninterrupted and endless, and when he finally opened his eyes he could not be sure that he had been or was not still dreaming.

He lay beneath a sheet on a luxuriously large bed in a beautifully decorated room, and he was naked beneath that sheet. His shoulder was bandaged and the arm was taped to his side. Lying beside him above the sheet and propped on to multiple pillows was a lovely young thing in the briefest of bikini panties and peekaboo shortie-top of purplish gauze; her face was angled away from him and all but buried in the pages of a book — but yeah, they were the same long legs that had stood over his bleeding body so many dreams ago.

At the far side of the room upon a table at an open window was something equally as interesting. He thought at first that it was a life-size statue or mannikin — maybe a female Buddha. Whatever it was, it was stony-naked and seated in a somewhat awkward pose, facing the open window, legs folded and drawn up under it, ivory skin gleamingly reflecting the sun's rays, head slightly bent, absolutely unmoving, absolutely stark staring beautiful.

Bolan was gazing at the still figure and trying to get a better focus when another girl entered the room and came directly to the foot of the bed to stare at him in unblinking appraisal. She was clad in a long gown with a bulky shorter overgarment, maybe twenty-five or twenty-six, dark hair styled in a soft contour of the very lovely head, sensitive lips, eyes beautifully delineated and tending to brood a bit. Bolan returned her level gaze and presently she broke the silence. 'Welcome back to the world of light and beauty.'

He said, 'Is that what world this is?'

She solemnly nodded her head but whatever she had at the tip of her tongue was lost as the girl beside Bolan came out of her book and twisted toward him with a stifled little gurgle of excitement. 'You're back!' she squealed.

Bolan recognized the voice. It was one of the last things he'd heard before he died, or passed out, or whatever. He shifted his reluctant focus toward her and weakly asked, 'Where've I been?'

'Out of it,' she told him. 'Absolutely out of it for nearly twenty-four hours.'

The tall girl at the foot of the bed said, 'I'll fix you something light to eat,' and went back the way she'd come, silent as a wraith.

'That's Paula Lindley,' the girl at his side informed him. 'She went almost all the way through nurse's training. You can thank *her* for fixing you up.'

'I'll do that,' Bolan murmured. His eyes had a new focus and his mind was lethargically cataloging the shareholder of his bed. She was a moppet, no more than nineteen or twenty, with luminously inquisitive eyes, gleaming golden hair looping down to softly rounded shoulders in two heavy braids, the cutey-pie face of a rapturously expectant romantic.

'We knew we didn't dare get a doctor for you,' the cutey-pie was telling him in that very alive voice of bursting excitement. 'We know who you are, you see.' She giggled.

'But you don't know who we are, do you. I'm Evie Clifford.' She pointed to the girl in the lotus position at the window. 'That's Rachel Silver. Doesn't she have a fantastic body? Don't mind her, she's a home naturalist.'

Bolan shook at the cobwebs connecting his brain tissues and muttered, 'A what?'

'A home nudist. Also she's hung up on Yoga and she's meditating right now. At times she'll sit the whole day through like that, right there, and you might as well talk to the wall. Some roommate.'

'I'll bet you have very attentive neighbors on the other side of that window,' Bolan commented sluggishly.

The moppet laughed and rolled her eyes. 'Yeah, I'll bet. But don't worry, no one saw us bring you in. We dress-carted you.'

'What?'

'We curled you up in the box of a dress cart, covered you with bolt ends, hung a bunch of fashions on the overhead rods, and just pushed you right through the whole mess, cops and everything.' Her eyes were dancing with the exciting memory. 'We thought we'd die when your blood started leaking out.'

Darkly Bolan said, 'Yeah, me too.' He heaved himself to a sitting position then quickly eased back to the pillow when the room began revolving about him.

'How long did you say I've been out?' he asked her, his voice suddenly going thick and guttural.

'Since two o'clock yesterday afternoon. This is Sunday, almost noon. Paula's been getting worried. She was thinking about trying to rent some I.V. equipment if you didn't come out of it pretty soon.'

'Rent what?' Bolan asked dizzily.

'You know the bottles and the tubes and needles and junk for intravenous feeding?'

'Oh.'

'So you'd better try eating whatever Paula brings you, unless you want to end up with a needle in the arm.'

Bolan closed his eyes and tried to piece things together in his mind.

The girl beside him was bubbling on. 'This is just like a

movie. Just wait 'till I write home about this, they'll never believe me. I was scared to death when I saw the cops in the basement but Rachel just kept whispering, "Push, Evie, push," and finally I got myself together and I said, "Right on," and boy we just whisked you out of there and into the van.'

Her voice dropped an octave and she was half-whispering as she added, 'Did you know that you slept with me all night?'

Bolan grinned, opened his eyes a slit, and lied. 'Sure, I knew it.'

A variety of emotions crossed the unsophisticatedly pretty face and after a brief silence she said, 'You're teasing me. You were out all the time.'

Drawing upon his 'dream,' Bolan told her, 'Not with those long legs wrapped around me, doll, I wasn't out *all* of the time.'

The girl's face turned a fiery red and she replied, 'Well I was probably doing that in *my* sleep, whatever you're talking about. I mean, I didn't lay here awake all night, you know. This *is* my bed. And Paula said you needed body therapy more than anything else. After all, I wouldn't attack a wounded man.'

From across the room came a coolly modulated voice. 'If you were in heat, Evie, you'd attack a wounded rhino.'

The girl giggled, tossed her head, and called back, 'I thought you were meditating.'

'I have been in *The One*,' the cool voice replied. She shifted about to peer over her shoulder, luminous eyes raking Bolan in a quick, see-all scrutiny. Bolan shivered. It was the face he had carried with him into paradise. 'I asked *One* for your life,' she informed him in a totally undramatic voice.

Bolan was beginning to decide that the dream had not ended. He heard himself asking the cool one, 'And what did *One* say to that?'

The girl twisted about to face him and dropped her legs

23

over the side of the table. They dangled, then crossed at the ankles, she smiled and brought her palms up even with her shoulders. 'You're alive, aren't you.'

'I guess,' Bolan replied, though he was not all that certain. He lay there and watched her slither off the table. She moved like a cat, all fluid and tawny grace, with the controlled springiness of superbly developed and coordinated muscles. The body was unbelievably exquisite, tight and hard looking yet entirely feminine with all the proper curves and angles in the right places. Her hair was shiny black and fell in a torrent to the small of her back where it clung. The tight flesh of her torso gleamed and rippled, and the motions of her body as she walked created the illusion that she was moving across shifting sand.

She reached the side of the bed and stood there smiling down at him with all the detachment of a Siamese cat. Bolan did not feel like smiling back. For some unaccountable reason, he felt like shouting something offensively obscene.

The sheeny black badge of puffy-soft feminity at the base of that ivory abdomen was at a direct level with his eyes, and it was to this that he directed his compulsive remark. He said, 'Hello, *One*. Okay, this is your life.'

Evie Clifford exploded into a fit of coughing and fell off the bed. The nude girl's eyes performed a rapid blinking sequence, then she silently spun on her heel to walk away. Bolan grabbed her hand and clung to it, squeezing with all his strength, which wasn't much.

'I don't know why I said that,' he murmured apologetically.

'I know why,' came the cool reply.

'Evie tells me that you helped bootleg me out of the grave. Thanks. And I'm sorry for the silly remark.'

'It's perfectly understandable,' she replied in a cold purr. 'And I'm the one who is sorry. For affronting your sense of modesty.' The girl disengaged her hand from his grip and glided from the room.

24

Evie Clifford's eyes appeared over the edge of the bed. 'Socko,' she whispered. 'Don't feel sorry, she had that coming. All this bilge about the holiness of the body. It's about time someone told her that hairy monkey between her thighs isn't all that holy to look at.'

'I didn't mean it that way,' Bolan muttered.

'You got the message across just the same.' The girl crawled on to the bed and knelt there staring at him with frank curiosity. 'Is it true that you've killed hundreds of men?'

Bolan returned her level gaze, then dropped his eyes to the perky little breasts peeking through the gauzy jacket. Surely he was either asleep or dead, in purgatory or some concoction of hell. The shoulder was beginning to pulse and he was suddenly feeling very weak. And yet he wanted a woman. He wanted a woman in the very worst way. Yes. He supposed that hell could be this way. He told the girl, 'There are worse things than killing.'

'I guess it depends on who you kill,' she replied solemnly.

Bolan shook his head doggedly, as though pleading his case before the keeper of heaven's gate. 'No matter who, there are worse things.'

'What, for instance?'

'*Not* killing, sometimes.'

She smiled winsomely and told him, 'I guess I don't get that. You should talk it over with Rachel. She's the deep one.' She giggled and added, 'Mentally, I mean. Physically, I think she's all glossy exterior. I bet she doesn't even have a vagina inside that monkey's mouth. I mean, I get that feeling sometimes. Know what I mean?'

Bolan hoped to God he did not know what she meant. That would *surely* be hell. And such statements issuing from that ingenuous face were just another irrational dimension of his mad dreaming. Surely. If it were not a dream, then he must have awakened to madness.

At that moment the tall efficient one reappeared with a tray. She set it on the bed, showed Bolan poached eggs and dry toast and let him sniff a cup of weak tea. 'You want to try this?' she asked him.

Yes, Bolan would try anything sane. He thanked her with his eyes and said, 'I believe I can handle it.'

She arranged the tray for his easy access, puffed the pillows behind him and helped him to a workable position, then watched attentively as he struggled through the self-feeding. As he ate, she told him, 'If you're wondering about your wounds, you got off pretty easy. There's a tiny furrow across your hip, no problem there. I dressed it with sulfa salve, just to take no chances with infection. As for your shoulder . . . well, you're a very lucky man. You lost an ounce of two of tissue, but nothing vital. If the bullet hadn't nicked a large artery, you'd probably still be out running the streets. But you lost a tremendous amount of blood. I've been worried about . . . well, you're obviously strong enough to fight back. You *are* a fighter, aren't you?'

Bolan grinned and said nothing, dizzily working at the elusive eggs.

'How long since you'd slept?' she prodded. 'I mean, before yesterday.'

He thought about it for a moment, then replied, 'I really don't remember. A couple of days, I guess.'

'Uh huh, that's what I thought. You're worn down, physically neglected, and you were probably reaching the edge of your reserves even if you hadn't been shot. I don't want you out of this bed for at least another two days.'

'You don't understand,' Bolan weakly protested. 'My enemies know their business. They'll track me here sooner or later, bet on that, and—'

'They've already been here,' Paula told him. 'Late last night. They went through here with a fine comb, so I'm sure they're satisfied. They won't be coming back.'

Bolan was giving her the uncomprehending stare.

She smiled and explained, 'We hid you in the bathtub. With Rachel.'

Bolan groaned inwardly. The dream, the damned dream. It was all coming back now. *All* of it had not been dream. He murmured, 'I don't know how to thank you girls.'

Evie Clifford laughed and told him, 'We'll think of something, I bet.'

'Yes, we'll think of something,' Paula assured him in solemn tones.

Somehow Bolan got the idea that the ladies had already thought of something. He mumbled an unintelligible response and pushed the tray away, then closed his eyes and cautiously maneuvered himself back to the horizontal position. The food had filled him with a numb warmth, and the black whirlpool was again summoning him.

As he drifted into the void, he heard Evie declare, 'Hey, he's passing out again.'

'That's fine,' came Paula's quiet voice, seemingly from far away.

'Well I can't lay here with this guy forever like this. He's tearing me up, just simply shredding me.'

'Okay, Hotsy,' was the crisp reply. 'Go on, I'll supply the body for a while. Tell Rachel to relieve me at four.'

Bolan distantly heard Evie sigh and leave the bed. Then the sheet was drawn back and something soft and warm moved in beside him, pressing close with sweet scents and cushiony resilience. Satiny arms worked him into a tender embrace and the smooth flesh of softly powerful legs intertwined his in full command. A fragment of something someone had said, '. . . body therapy . . .' drifted through his closing consciousness and he said, 'Yeah, I'll buy that,' but he did not know if the words left his throat or not.

'Take my strength,' whispered a soft voice. 'Body to body, lover, take it and build upon it.'

Yeah, yeah, here came the bottomless pit and Bolan was slipping into it, but it really didn't matter. It was all a mad dream in a madhouse, and the Executioner had freaked out for sure. Face to face, body to body, it was a total freakout.

CHAPTER THREE

CORPSES

BOLAN's recovery was dramatically quick under the constant ministrations of his three nurses. He was fed every time his eyes flickered open, and the bizarre 'body therapy' continued around the clock. On Monday he was up and prowling about under his own steam, getting the lie of the luxury apartment shared by the girls. It appeared that they had no money problems. The building was located in the high rise and high rent district of Manhattan's fashionable East Side. The apartment was one of those garden terrace setups with the ultra-modern decor which is usually associated with modest wealth. There were but two bedrooms, one of which was shared by the moppet and the Yogi. Paula had the other one to herself, but Bolan considered it quite a sacrifice for personal privacy – very small, windowless, with hardly space enough to walk around the bed.

Most of the apartment was given over to a split-level and luxuriously appointed living area, quite spacious and supplying just about every conceivable animal comfort – from a glassed-in massage and sun lamp den to a swinging bar with built-in entertainment center. The kitchen wasn't overly much, but fully gadgeted and probably adequate for a trio of working girls who perhaps confined their food preparations to dry salads and black coffee. The refrigerator now was amply stocked with gobs of red beef, brought in especially for consignment to Bolan's blood-building chemistry.

Thanks to the compulsive talker, Bolan had learned that Paul's age was twenty-six, making her the eldest of the three and obviously a sort of den mother. Rachel was twenty-two, Evie twenty. The girls shared an equal interest in *Paula's Fashions*. The fashion design know-how belonged to Paula, Rachel had brought local fame and following as a model, Evie the cash. They had a going enterprise, concentrating on the far-out learnings of the freaky set and, according to Evie, outshining all the competition in that field.

Bolan had been informed, that morning, that the 'body therapy' routine was *finis*. As he understood it, the idea was a pet theory of Paula's which she had picked up from some Eastern mystic, having something to do with the flow of life energies from body to body. She explained to Bolan,

'The basis of all universal laws is the principle of balance. Our universe is balanced, the planets and the stars all giving off and receiving energies from one another, and our bodies do the same thing. A body with an ebbing life force will naturally induct the stronger energies emanating from a proximate body. This practice of isolating the sick with the sick is primitive hogwash and it's self-defeating. Every sick person should go to bed with a strong, healthy partner – someone who can spare a slight diminishing of their own vital energies. The value gained by the vital forces of the patient could easily mean the difference between life and death.'

Bolan could understand why she had not completed her nurse's training. 'Yeah, but something else gets vitalized in the process,' he pointed out, 'and a guy could end up losing a lot more energy than he gained.'

'That's why we are discontinuing your body therapy,' Paula explained. Her eyes flashed mischievously. 'Anyway, libidinal energies are the strongest force the body has going for it. Yours seem to be fully restored, so you've disqualified yourself from further body therapy.'

It was the nuttiest quackery Bolan had ever heard, but he kept a straight face and let the matter drop. They had saved his life; he would not openly question their methods. Something had worked, certainly.

29

Paula and Evie had gone off to keep the goldmine in operation, leaving Rachel to babysit the mending houseguest. Bolan had been trying, without apparent success, to penetrate the aloof coolness of the beauteous nursemaid and to repair the lines of communication he had so thoughtlessly ripped asunder on that first encounter. He had not seen the girl without clothing since that awful moment, or at least without what would pass for clothing in any nudist camp. At the moment she wore buckskin hotpants which hugged the hips, deeply plunging at front and rear, and with cutouts that revealed a goodly area of shiny buttock to each side. A fringed leather thingamajig hung from some hidden suspension point across the bountiful chest – like a Kit Carson fringed jacket without the jacket. A narrow headband with a tiny oriental symbol of some sort traversed the forehead just above the eyes to complete the ensemble.

Bolan asked her, 'Is that one of Paula's designs?'

She shook her head in that feline way and replied, 'No, I conceived this myself.'

Bolan grinned. 'Your concession to prudery,' he suggested quietly.

Her eyes flashed to his, then skittered away. 'There is nothing vulgar about the human body. I simply want to get that into the record. Vulgarity is a mental creation.'

Bolan asked her, 'Did you pull that discovery out of *The One*?'

'Don't joke about that,' she warned him. 'There are many names for God.'

Hell, Bolan thought, *a nudist holy roller*. Aloud, he replied, 'Sorry, I didn't realize you took it so seriously.'

'I take it very seriously,' she assured him.

'Why don't you just call him *God*?'

'The word is too fraught with superstitious ignorance. Words are very important, don't you think? They are symbols of our mental content.'

He told her, 'I guess you're right. So what sort of symbol pops out when I'm thinking about sex?'

She watched him warily for a moment, then replied, 'I don't know about you. For me, the word is *purity*.'

'Purity,' he echoed, sliding the word through his mind for size. 'Sorry, the ideas seem to clash.'

'In your mind, yes, because you think in vulgar terms. You kill, and you terrorize, and you thump your chest like a jungle ape, and of course you take your sex in the same frame of mind.'

She was striking back, and Bolan was finding it uncomfortable. He told her, 'My killing and my sexing have no connection at all. I don't want a fight with you, Rachel. But I'm curious. In what frame of mind do you take your sex?'

'I do not take sex,' she replied coolly.

'All right,' he said, thoroughly subdued.

'It takes me,' she explained.

'Oh.'

'This is the only purity, you see. A man and woman meet, something sparks between them, and sex immediately takes them if they are wise.'

Chuckling, he asked, 'You mean they just flop down immediately and let sex take it, wherever they may be when the sparks fly, on the sidewalk at Times Square or on the floor of the Brooklyn subway.'

She smiled and told him, 'You're thumping your chest again. It's not necessary to "flop down" anywhere. For the wise, it is enough to merely let sex take you, and lead you to the proper time and place.'

He did not even wish to mull that one over. 'And if you're not wise?' he prompted her.

'Then you fall into impurity, into vulgarity, seductive maneuvers, thinly covered repressions, with nothing left of the pure impulse but lecherous thoughts and dishonest actions. It is the birth of pornography. We sparked, Mack

31

Bolan, you and I, yesterday. And you flung my spark back into my face.'

That was not, Bolan was thinking, where he had flung it – and indeed he had not known even what he had been flinging. So now he knew.

He solemnly told her, 'I wasn't even half here yesterday, Rachel.'

'I know. Even so, you flung me into impurity.'

The girl swayed away and left him sitting there staring out the window onto a crisp December day. It was a conversation he would not forget, but now he tucked it away for future reference. There were more pressing puzzles to think about. For openers, how long could he expect to sponge on the generosity and good nature of his hostesses? To how much danger was he exposing them by his mere presence there? And what sort of city-shaking gyrations was the mob putting itself through for Bolan's head? And how about the cops? Were they all just sitting back and waiting for him to show? He doubted it.

The answers to those questions were, of course, opproaching critical mass. He realized in a flash, then, that the talk with Rachel Silver did have a bearing on his own mode of living. She had been speaking of sex and purity, but the application for Bolan was *warfare* and purity. There *was* purity in warfare. A hellish kind of purity. An army gets soft and undisciplined when it's off the line; the same truth applied equally to a lone warrior. Each moment that he remained in this R and R camp, he knew, he was falling that much farther into gross impurity.

He had to get back on the line. The sooner the better. He got up, carefully made his way to the bathroom, unbandaged his wound, and stood in front of the mirror to inspect it. Paula's stitches were a bit uneven and raggedy-ended, but the flesh surrounding them seemed healthy and alive. He guessed she'd known what she was doing. Then he glanced at his face. A two-day accumulation of whiskers was already radically altering his appearance. He would let them grow, he decided, and try to hang on with the girls for a couple more days, at least until the wobbles left his legs. Then he for damn sure had to get back on the line. A war awaited him.

On Tuesday morning, Bolan rolled off the couch to which he had been unceremoniously deported the previous evening and was delighted to find that he could walk swiftly across the room without becoming dizzy. A bit of bounce had returned to his step and he could lift the left arm to shoulder level with only a moderate degree of agony. He consumed a twenty-ounce steak from Paula's grill and confessed to her that he felt 'ready to rassle a grizzly'.

Perhaps because of that remark, Paula decided that Bolan should be left alone thenceforth, at least during the working day, and all three girls were packed off to the salon. Evie darted back into the apartment to hang a moist kiss on Bolan's lips and whisper, 'Don't go way, huh?'

Bolan grinned and shooed her back out. Alone for the first time in days, he took a lingering shower and then gingerly tested his shoulder with a series of limbering-up exercises.

Later that morning, Paula took time from her busy schedule to go to the East Side Air Terminal and claim Bolan's luggage. She delivered it to him and found him performing push-ups on the living room floor and gritting his teeth against the pain in the shoulder.

'I guess you know what you're doing,' she told him, and hurried back out.

Bolan knew precisely what he was doing. He had to get that shoulder functioning, and quickly. Some deeply welling instinct had been working at him all morning; he knew that his time had come.

He took the bag into the large bedroom and opened it, then immediately checked the false bottom. It was intact, and so were the contents – the hot little 9mm Beretta automatic he'd picked up in France, plus the sideleather and a stack of spare clips. He double-checked the Beretta's action, then slid in a clip and chambered in a round at the ready, hesitated momentarily, then added the silencer to the muzzle and carefully installed the piece in the sideleather. Then he got into fresh clothing and buckled on the shoulder rig, wincing and readjusting the strap to clear his wound.

He left the bag lying open on the bed and carried his jacket into the living room, seeking pencil and paper to leave a note for the girls.

A small wall secretary occupied a spot just off the L-shaped foyer. It was here that Bolan was headed when the front door swung open and a guy in a brown suit stepped into the apartment. He was holding one of those clever little sliding-blade door-jimmies and softly chuckling to himself with some secret joke, and he was more upset than Bolan by the surprise encounter. The chuckle died in his throat and his eyes were bulging at the display of gunleather crossing Bolan's chest. The jimmy slipped through his fingers and he made a fumbling move toward the inside of his jacket.

Bolan's Beretta cleared leather much quicker and he commanded, 'Freeze!'

Brownsuit froze and gawked and stuttered, 'Wh-what the h-hell is this?'

Bolan said, 'You tell me.'

'Police,' the guy squawked. 'I'm a policeman.'

'Prove it.'

The intruder showed Bolan a sick smile and nothing else. 'So I'm not,' he admitted. The look in Bolan's eyes turned the smile somewhat sicker and he added, 'I didn't expect to find you here, Bolan. Not standin' on both feet, anyhow.'

'I guess not,' Bolan said coldly. They stood there silently staring at each other for a moment, then Bolan told him, 'When you stop talking, soldier, you stop living.'

Brownsuit's mouth opened and closed a couple of times before the words started, then they fell in a torrent. 'Sammie had us staking out th' baggage room down at East Side. We had a man in back. You know. Watching the bags from Kennedy, the ones that came in Saturday. We been checkin' all of 'em, and this was the last one left. This broad comes in and got it and we tailed her here. That's all, Bolan. Christ, I ain't no triggerman.'

'You're with Sam the Bomber,' Bolan reminded him.

The guy nodded vehemently and said, 'Yeah, but not like you think. Only temporary, I'm on loan from Jake Sacarelli. I run girls over in Brooklyn. I never got in on no contract before.'

'So you've fumbled your big chance, soldier.'

The guy's eyes were getting frantic. He said, 'Christ, I was just following the baggage, that's all.'

'You and who else?'

'Me'n Tony Boy Laccardo.'

'And where is Tony Boy now?'

'He's waiting down by the elevator, just down th' hall.'

Bolan nodded curtly and asked, 'Okay, and who else?'

Brownsuit swallowed hard and replied, 'We got a wheelman waitin' down at the curb.'

'What kind of car?'

'Chivvy, I think. Yeah. A blue Chivvy.'

Bolan commanded, 'Finish pulling that gun out, but use the other hand, and just let me see two fingers. Pull it out and set it down easy.'

The *Mafioso* complied, then quickly straightened up and croaked, 'Christ, don't wipe me, Bolan. I got nothin' against you personal.'

'Who knows you came here, other than your two partners?'

Brownsuit must have thought he saw a glimmer of hope. He quickly replied, 'Nobody else, I swear. We been watchin' those damn bags since Saturday. We really didn't expect no payoff, it was gettin' to be a drag. Nobody knows, Bolan. And I got nothin' personal against you. Lemme go, huh? I mean, wing me or something if you think you gotta, but Christ don't cut me down cold, Bolan.'

This was the part of warfare which Bolan thoroughly hated. No man went willingly to his death, no one was ever quite prepared for the cold and utter finality of that moment, especially when he was standing there helplessly waiting for it. Bolan did not like to kill cold.

But his dilemma reminded him again of the cool words of Rachel Silver, about not taking sex but rather allowing sex to take her. To Rachel, that was purity. Well, there was purity in warfare too. A good soldier, likewise, did not take war; he let war take him. An impure or unwise soldier became just another dishonest politician, or gouging businessman, or something worse. Still — Bolan found himself squirming under his distasteful duty.

Of course, if Brownsuit had walked in and found Bolan lying half dead and helpless in bed, he would have finished him off without a qualm, and then he would probably have hacked off Bolan's head with a penknife and carried it proudly to the *Commissione* in a paper sack. Even so, if this were simply a case of Bolan versus the pleading *Mafioso*, he would not feel so compelled to kill. It was highly important, though, to Paula Lindley and her roommates that this man die. Bolan knew what would happen to the girls if this guy walked out alive. Their lives would not be worth a nickel.

Bolan told the brownsuited pimp from Brooklyn, 'I've nothing personal against you either, soldier,' the Beretta phutted softly through its silencer and Brownsuit died without even knowing it, a high-velocity Parabellum angling in through the bridge of the nose and displaying several cubic inches of brain tissue in painless and instant death. If Bolan had to kill cold, this was the way he preferred.

He pulled the suitcoat up over the guy's head and stuffed in a small throw-pillow to lessen the spread of blood, tying the bundle into place with the coatsleeves. Then he put on his own jacket and stepped over the body for a *tête-à-tête* with Tony Boy Laccardo, 'just down th' hall'.

He found him there, and killed him there, without a word

36

and without a warning, as Tony Boy raised surprised eyes from a racing form. Bolan shoved the remains into a janitor's closet where he found a huge mop with which he sponged up the pool of blood on the floor of the hallway. Then he returned to the apartment, transferred Brownsuit to the same dress cart which had brought Bolan there, and he stopped off at the janitor's closet for a quick pickup of Tony Boy. He tossed the mop in too, covered the bodies with rags from the closet shelf, and took his cargo into the elevator down to the garage.

A dull-faced attendant glanced at Bolan without curiosity as he wheeled the cart to a loading dock near the exit.

Bolan yelled over to him, 'I gotta bring my car in.'

The attendant moved his head in a bored nod and went back to his funny book or whatever he was reading.

Bolan went out and proceeded unhurriedly to the corner of the building, then along the front toward a waiting blue Chevrolet idling in a no-parking zone at the curb. He approached from the rear, opened the right-front door, and slid in beside the wheelman. The guy did a double take on his unexpected guest, the eyes freezing still on the Beretta.

An icy voice told him, 'I want Sam the Bomber's address, and I want it with no shitting around.'

The wheelman's voice came choked and ragged and with no shitting around as he replied, 'Look in the glove box, I think there's some cards.'

Bolan looked and found a thin stack of business cards, embossed with Chianti's name in fancy gold lettering and the interesting announcement: *Human Engineering Contractor*. Bolan found that almost funny, but he pocketed one of the cards and slammed the door on the glove compartment with no show of humor and told his temporary companion, 'Okay, let's roll. Around the building and to the garage entrance, west side.' He restrained the driver for a moment to pull a small caliber pistol out of the man's waist band and toss it into the back seat, then he waggled a

37

finger at the wheelman and the vehicle lurched forward.

Moments later they were easing into the underground garage and backing to the loading ramp. Bolan took the keys from the ignition, pushing the man out and slid out behind him, then handed him the keys and commanded, 'Open the trunk.'

The wheelman meekly accepted the keys then went reluctantly to the rear of the car, his eyes searching for some hint of help in the offing but finding nothing of comfort. The only other sign of human presence was the attendant in the little glassed-in office, hunched over his desk and utterly absorbed in something there.

Bolan leapt onto the dock and positioned the cart with his foot, then told the wheelman, 'Get up here.'

The *Mafioso* gave Bolan a questioning look, but did as he was told without overt challenge to that indisputable authority, even though the Beretta was no longer in view. He joined his captor and awaited further instructions.

They came coldly and simply. 'Clean that junk out of my cart.'

The man shrugged and seized a hand full of rags and tossed them into the trunk of the car. Then he saw the blood on his hands, and his knees buckled and he almost fell. Calmly the death voice commanded, 'All of it!'

The guy already knew what was beneath the remaining rags. He shivered and clawed them away from the corpses, then quickly averted his gaze and whispered, 'My God, oh my God.'

Bolan's jacket opened and the Beretta peered out at the shaken man. 'You've got about one heartbeat to get busy, soldier.'

The man nodded and sent furtive glances in all directions, then leaned into the cart and lifted out Tony Boy and set him in the trunk with a distasteful grunt. Brownsuit was a bit heavier and the wheelman's legs were going rubbery on him. Bolan lent a hand and they got the big man fitted in

38

atop Tony Boy, then Bolan put his prisoner to work mopping out the cart. When the job was finished, the bloody rags and the soggy mop went into the trunk over Brownsuit and Tony Boy, and Bolan told the wheelman, 'Okay, you too. Get in there.'

The guy's face went dead white and he gurgled, 'God no, not that, don't make me get in *there*!'

Bolan told him, 'You won't mind,' and phutted a painless Parabellum through an eyesocket. The guy fell over into the trunk and Bolan helped him stay there, shoving him on in beside his companions and doubling the legs over to clear the latching mechanism.

A muscle twitched in his jaw and he muttered, 'Pure war, Rachel, is pure hell. How are *you* making out?'

Then he closed the trunk and returned the dress cart to the apartment. Moments later he was behind the wheel of the blue Chevrolet and tooling out of the garage. The attendant looked up and nodded at him as he passed, and Bolan waved.

He pulled out into the street. He took out Chianti's business card for another look at the address engraved thereon, then he grunted and swung north towards the Triborough Bridge. He did not know the Bronx too well, but he would find Sam the Bomber Chianti, and he would deliver this hot shipment of rapidly cooling cargo.

Corpses were something that Sam the Bomber would understand. He had trafficked in them for almost as long as Mack Bolan had been alive.

Sam was going to discover, though, that the supply was beginning to greatly exceed the demand.

And he was going to discover that damned quick.

CHAPTER FOUR

ENGINEERS

SAM THE BOMBER began his climb to underworld prominence in the early 1940's, in a nation at war and suffering the inconvenience of a rationing of vital commodities — things such as butter, meat, gasoline, tires, sugar, coffee, and many luxury items. Commodity rationing was one of the minor hardships of a world at war, to be sure, but many Americans could not accept even this small sacrifice to national survival. Instead, they made rich men out of petty crooks by satisfying their selfish appetites with black market purchases of stolen commodities and/or stolen or counterfeit ration coupons. So proliferate were these black markets in wartime scarcities that rival marketeers in some areas of the nation engaged one another in territorial contests and gang wars to equal the bloody battles of the prohibition era. The American Mafia, ever alert to the smell of quick money, lost no time in dominating this lucrative side-effect of the war, and neighborhood punks like Sam Chianti found readymade careers awaiting them in this 'little world war' of black market racketeering.

Chianti pulled his first muscle job at the age of sixteen, when he threw a fire bomb into an automobile repair garage belonging to one Adolph Bruhman, a small time Bronx businessman who refused to honor black market gasoline coupons for unlimited sales to customers of Freddie Gambella, then an obscure underling in the Mavnarola Family. That fire bomb killed Bruhman, three employees, and two customers — and endeared the precocious hoodlum to Gambella, who was already busily establishing himself in the line of succession to Mavnarola's crown. Little Sammy Chianti, seventh grade dropout and neighborhood terrorist, became known as Sam the Bomber and participated in another fifty-six slayings before attaining legal age. He was adjudged sub-intelligent and unfit for military service by his local draft board in 1944 and again in 1946, but he was intelligent enough to repeatedly break virtually every law of his society over a period of some thirty years without once being convicted of a major crime. And he possessed intelligence enough to remain alive and viable in the ever-shifting structure and fortunes of the New York underworld and, moreover, to establish himself as a respected and honored member of that structure. Perhaps the patronage of Freddie Gambella contributed to this 'success' story – but the fact remains that Sam the Bomber had been a professional killer for thirty years and had never spent a night in jail.

Now forty-six years of age, Chianti had long ago come to the realization that he 'had it made'. No longer required to directly participate in the mob's muscle departments, Sam the Bomber sat in a swank office in the front of his Bronx home, a restored two-story brownstone in a modest neighborhood of identical restorations, pushing buttons that sent extortion, hard persuasion, and frequently death into the midst of his community. Sam was 'a contractor's contractor', a muscle-and-gun business built and preserved by rockbed reliability and guaranteed results. Though without official rank in the organization, he enjoyed the friendship and camaraderie of various chieftains, lieutenants, and enforcers of all the five families of New York – plus a reputation which was respected throughout the sprawling syndicate. Freddie Gambella was the godfather of Sam's two kids, and their wives had been close pals since Sam's marriage in 1951. So who needed formal rank when self-evident rank was draped all over him? Sam had no ambitions to ever become a *Capo*; it was more than enough that *Capos* sought his advice and accepted his hospitality and kept making him richer and richer.

Sure, Sam the Bomber had it made. So why, he was wondering on that cold December day in the Bronx, had he felt compelled to get out there on the streets again, after all these years of 'softing it', and make a total ass of himself? Over-anxiety, he supposed. Bolan was a big fish. A hundred grand worth of fish, not to mention the immeasurable value in prestige for the contractor who landed him. It had been a natural thing, Sam decided, for him to go out personally on a job like that one. After all, the biggest guns in the syndicate had been blasting at that guy for months now. Boys like the Talifero brothers, Quick Tony Lavagni, Sam's old buddy Danno Giliamo, Nick Trigger, and a host of others – most of them dead now.

Sam was certain that he was the luckiest man alive to even *be* alive. Not many had stood eye to eye with that Bolan bastard, and fumbled, and came away to tell about it – or try to live it down – no, not many. The guy was no punk, he was no ordinary street pigeon, hell no. Sam had gone up against some pretty tough numbers in his time, some pretty damn *deadly* numbers – but he had never faced such cold and awful deadliness in his whole life as he faced that terrible Saturday out at Kennedy. Hell no. That son of a bitch could stare down a pissed-off rattler. Jesus he had never seen such eyes in his whole life. No wonder Sam got rattled.

But Sam was more than just rattled, and he recognized that. He'd been a long time off the streets, his kids were in the fanciest boarding schools in the East, and his old lady hadn't touched a dirty dish or a Monday wash in all the years they'd been married. Everybody had known that Sam Chianti had it made. Sam had known it too. Until Saturday. Yeah, Sam had gotten more than a rattling. Everything he had was a result of his reputation with a contract, and Sam had suddenly been made to feel very insecure. Word was out an hour after it happened, all over town, Sam the Bomber had personally muffed a contract. It might seem like a small thing to some people, but when a guy lived off a reputation, then the first tiny crack in that reputation could be like the crack in a dam, the whole thing could fall to hell in an awful hurry.

It was funny, he was thinking, he hadn't been a damn bit afraid of Bolan, not a damn bit, even knowing what the bastard had been doing all this time to the biggest guns in the business. Sam the Bomber had been bigger than Mack the bastard Bolan, he'd been ten feet bigger and he hadn't been afraid of that jerk. Now he was. He had to face it. He was afraid.

He stared at his reflection in the glossy surface of the huge mahogany desk and admitted it to himself, straight out. If something didn't happen pretty fast, if his crews couldn't get a line on the bastard pretty soon . . . Well, Sam hated to face such an eventuality. He didn't have to face it. He'd built a business and a gilt-edged reputation on finding people and doing things for them. He had his contacts, Sam had thirty damn years of contacts, know-how and people spread everywhere in this town, every borough, every precinct – sooner or later he would find this bastard Bolan. Sooner, he fervently hoped.

Hell, maybe the guy was dead. He'd been bleeding like a stuck pig, Jesus how much blood could a guy lose and still keep going? Maybe the cops had him on ice in some morgue all this time, keeping the secret and just waiting for the organization to do something dumb. Maybe . . .

Chianti picked up a pencil and hurled it across the office. Maybe *shit*! You didn't close contracts on *maybe's*. At that moment the telephone rang. He stared at it and let it sound twice more, then he grabbed it up and gave a guarded, 'Yeah?'

'Sam, this is Fred,' came a troubled voice.

The boss, his buddy, godfather to his kids, Sam this is Fred, in a tone of voice that might as well have said Sam you

43

shithead what the fuck are you doing about this fucking contract you shithead you.

He swallowed past a sudden lump in his throat and said, 'Glad you called, Freddie. Listen, I think I got that man you wanted.'

Another Sam, over in Jersey, had gone through some embarrassing shit just recently over a tapped phone, this Sam wasn't having any of that. 'Three of my engineers are out now interviewing a likely candidate.'

'Yeah?' asked Sam this is Fred.

'Yeah. They made a contact over at East Side this morning. My representative there phoned about an hour ago, maybe an hour-and-a-half, to say they'd come across something interesting. I think maybe we got your man.'

'Well I hope so, Sam,' was the drawling response. 'My board of directors are getting pretty damned edgy over this thing. They seem to think that three days is plenty enough time to at least make a contact. You know what I mean, Sam. They get nervous when these things just drag on and no word ever comes back.'

'They'll be getting some word pretty damn quick,' Chianti assured his *Capo*. 'I'll lay my whole reputation on that, Freddie.'

'It's already there, Sam.'

Chianti swallowed again and said, 'Yeah, I guess it is.'

'By the way, our attorneys say you can rest easy about those engineers that, uh, you know got detained on that legal matter the other day. He says they'll be back to work tomorrow.'

'Oh great, I'm glad to hear that.' Bullshit, who gave a damn about the dumb pricks who had no better sense than to get theirselves arrested like a bunch of punks. They should've known better than . . .

'Well, we'll be waiting to hear about this latest contact, Sam. With the greatest interest. Don't let us down, eh?'

'You know I won't, Freddie,' Chianti told the *Capo*.

'Give my regards to Theresa. Oh yeah, Marie wants to know about the card game tonight. You know, considering the business pressures and all, what d'you think? Should we call it off?'

'I guess we better, Freddie. I got too much on my mind.'

'Yeah, well, we'll try to make it for next Tuesday then.'

'Sure, things ought to be more relaxed by then.'

'I guess they'll have to be, Sam. See you.'

Chianti whispered, 'See you,' to a dead line and woodenly returned the instrument to its base. Okay, sure, he'd known it, that was how things went. From one tiny crack to a goddamned flood. Now Freddie was calling off the damned ritual card game, that tore it all, Sam the Bomber could damn well see the handwriting on the wall now. Jesus he *had* to get Bolan, there wasn't no other way, Sam's whole life hung on it.

He nervously lit a cigar and, immersed in his thoughts, forgot to keep it going. It went out and he lit it again. It went out again and he heaved it across the room. Then Angelo Totti, the big bodyguard, rapped lightly on the door and poked his head inside and said, 'You got a minute, boss?'

The boss's response was uncharacteristically petulant. 'Hell that's all I have got. What the hell is it now, Angelo?'

The big man came into the room, swinging a set of car keys in front of his face. 'There's a kid out here, brought these keys in, says they're yours.'

Chianti squinted at the keys, then held out his hand for them. Totti surrendered them and watched interestedly as Chianti examined them. 'These go to one of our leased cars,' Chianti decided. 'What kid did you say?'

'This kid outside here,' the bodyguard replied, jerking a thumb at the door. 'Neighborhood punk, I seen 'im around before. He got one of your cards too, and something in a little brown envelope. Says he's gotta give it to you personal.'

45

Chianti got to his feet and went to the door. A boy of about fifteen was leaning against the wall of the outer office, whistling softly under his breath and ogling the swank decor.

Chianti barked at him, 'Where'd you get these keys, kid?'

'Guy outside,' the boy replied with obvious nervousness. 'Guy in a blue Chivvy. He parked the car out there and gave me the keys. Told me to bring 'em in.' He glanced at a business card in his hand. 'Are you Mr. Chianti?'

'Course I'm Mr. Chianti,' the contractor growled. He crossed to the door and peered out through the glass port-hole. Sure as hell, the car was parked over there across the street.

'Well I got this for you too.' The boy was extending a brown envelope.

Chianti reached for it and the boy jerked it back. 'The guy told me to collect twenty bucks.'

'What the hell for?'

'He just told me to make you give me twenty bucks.'

The thing was becoming humorous to the contractor's contractor. He pulled a bill out of his wallet and said, 'Okay, I'll tell you what we'll do. I'll lay the twenty bucks on this table here. You put the envelope down there. Then if you can pick up the twenty without getting your arm broke, then it's yours.'

The boy dropped the envelope and snatched the money in one lightning motion, jerked the door open, and was gone. Chianti was laughing and Totti said, 'You want me to get it back, boss?'

'Naw, Jesus the kid has guts, let him have it.' He picked up the small envelope and said, 'Now I wonder what . . .?'

The envelope came open and a small metallic object fell into Chianti's palm. His eyes raised in bafflement to his bodyguard's face and he grunted, 'A marksman's medal. Now what the hell . . .?' Then the bafflement turned to something else and the color left his face.

46

In an awed voice, Totti declared, 'That's Bolan's calling card. They say he leaves those things on—'

'I know what it is!' Chianti screeched.

The bodyguard strode to the door and threw it open.

Chianti yelled, 'Shut that goddamn door!' and ran into his office.

Totti did as he was told and followed his boss inside. Sam the Bomber was standing carefully at the wall near the front window and peering through a slit in the venetian blind.

In a half-stifled voice he said, 'I don't see nothing. Look . . . go back and get Ernie and Nate. Then go out there and check that car out. No. You stay with me. Give Ernie the keys. Tell 'im to be careful.'

Totti jerked his head in an understanding nod and hurried out.

This had to be the living end, the contractor's contractor was thinking. The son of a bitch had come to *them*. Sam almost had to admire that. He also had to fear it. And why not? There was something very bizarre and downright spooky about a fox that whistled at hounds. A fox, especially, with a six-figure bounty on his pelt.

Bolan was watching from a rooftop several doors down and across the street from the Chianti residence. The neighborhood told Bolan quite a bit about his prey. Sam the Bomber had grown up in this district, and he had seldom ventured more than fifty miles in any direction out of it. Here he was a big fish in a small pond, a local boy made good, and here he felt secure in a familiar environment which he had learned to manipulate to his own advantage. Yes, this told Bolan quite a bit about Sam Chianti.

He grinned when he saw the boy come flying out the front door with a scrap of green clutched in his hand. Bolan had been right about that item, also. Tomorrow Sam might drown the boy's father in the East River and terrorize his mother into white slavery, but today he would play the benign neighborhood patriarch and let the kid con him out of some pocket change because it was good for the image. Yeah, Bolan had known a hundred Sam the Bombers.

Now Bolan lay on the back side of the peaked roof and watched two nervous soldiers come slowly out of the house, peer up and down the street, and cross over to the blue Chevrolet. They walked around it, stared through the windows, and walked around it again. Then the heavy one stood in the street and nervously scanned the neighborhood while the other one, a tall skinny guy raised the hood and peered at the engine. Bolan smiled. They were looking for a bomb. The skinny one slipped under the car on his back and emerged a couple of minutes later at the rear. He got up and brushed off his clothes, then sent a hand signal to someone watching from inside the house.

The chubby one stepped up to the vehicle and opened the door on the passenger's side. He leaned inside, jerked quickly back out, said something to the skinny soldier, and snatched open the rear door to scoop something off the seat.

They had found the wheelman's revolver. Now they stood in a tight huddle and the skinny one was jerking his head in some emphatic argument, then he took something from the other man – the pistol, Bolan supposed – and ran across to the house and went inside. A moment later he re-emerged with another guy in tow, a huge man with shoulders like a lumberjack and overdeveloped pectoral muscles which caused his arms to swing like an ape as he walked.

The chubby one, meanwhile, had gone to the rear of the vehicle and was just standing there contemplating the trunk door. He said something to the other two as they approached. The musclebound newcomer leaned into the passenger compartment and the skinny guy went to the rear and fitted the key into the trunk door.

Bolan's angle of vision was from above and to the rear of the vehicle. He could not see the men's faces as that trunk lid raised, but he had no trouble seeing the overall reaction to their discovery there. Both of them stiffened and staggered back a step or two, with all the precision of carefully rehearsed choreography, and one of them let out a loud yelp.

The big guy leapt clear of the passenger compartment, hardware now visible in his hand, and moved with surprising agility to join the other two. He saw, and also reacted violently, lunging immediately forward to get both big paws inside there for a tactile verification of what his eyes were telling him. Then he straightened up and turned a frozen stare toward the Chianti residence. A door cracked open over there and a peevish voice called out, 'Well what the hell is it?'

The heavyweight yelled back, 'It's them three engineers from Brooklyn, or what's left of 'em.'

The door at the house immediately clicked shut. That decided Bolan's course of action. He grimaced and eased the Beretta up, clamping down on the peak of the roof with his armpit, letting his elbow find comfortable support on the opposite downslope. He had already calculated the firing range at roughly twenty yards. Ordinarily this would be an ideal range for the Beretta – he had worked it in with consistent two-inch groupings at twenty-five yards, pretty accurate for a handgun – but now he had to calculate the effect of the silencer on muzzle velocity and track deviation. And he definitely wanted that silencer in operation, especially now that Sam the Bomber was obviously not going to expose himself. Bolan had not really counted on getting Chianti this time, anyway. It would be enough, for now, to rattle his teeth a bit. And whispering death, Bolan had found, had a peculiar psychological effect on Mafia hardmen.

He was sighting down the short range now, allowing for gross error through the silencer, and knowing that he would have to get all three in rapid fire if he was to get them at all. They were still clumped at the rear of the vehicle, the heavyweight continuing to stare toward the house, the other two darting nervous glances into the bloody trunk.

Bolan fired once, twice, three times in quick succession – the 9mm Parabellums singing down to the street on slightly diverging paths and each finding solid-soft matter to stop their travel.

The heavyweight yelled something in a twangy falsetto and pitched forward with both hands scrabbling for the raised trunk door, then he fell away at the side and rolled onto his back. The other two had gone down without a sound, the skinny one crumpling onto the rear bumper and hanging there, his clothing apparently caught on something; the thick one folding down on rubber legs to sprawl face down in the street.

Bolan was not yet done with the Human Engineering Contractors. The Beretta angled toward the far side of the street and continued its abrupt little coughs. The big picture window fronting Chianti's office began sprouting a rash of round holes, then shattered with a loud crash. An instant later, the glass porthole of the massive door exploded inwardly.

And then Bolan was done. He released his grip on the peak and slid slowly down the far side of the roof, throwing in a fresh clip in a rapid re-load of the Beretta as he went and taking care to favor the bad shoulder. *That's twice, Sam,* he was saying to himself. *The third time around will be all for you.*

Across the way, Sam the Bomber was lying face down on his office carpet in a sea of shattered glass and wondering if he was shot or just cut up. Numbly he realized that he had not even seen the bastard, had not even heard any gunshots. Where the hell had the guy been firing from? All Sam had seen was his boys toppling over like rubber toys deflating, then *wham* and Sam's whole damn world was exploding around him.

This was going to look bad, damned bad. The word would be all over town now that Bolan was doing a job of human engineering on the contractor's contractor, and that was going to look bad as hell. That, he knew, was going to be the big crack in the dam of Sam the Bomber's life's work. He was being engineered by one hell of an engineer.

Well ... at least now he could call Freddie and tell him that he'd made that contact. Yeah, he sure had made that contact.

CHAPTER FIVE

PURITY

BOLAN'S withdrawal from the scene of combat was via the public transportation system. When he left the subway at 125th and Lenox, he hopped a bus to 110th and walked into East Harlem. According to his poop book, he would find an enterprising businessman there by the name of William Meyer who sold *objects de la guerre* at reasonable prices and without questions.

He found Meyer in a little machine shop in an alley behind a bakery, and it took no more than a minute or two for the arms expert to decide that young Meyer knew his business. The guy was an ex-GI and an armorer like Bolan – but, unlike Bolan, completely warred-out and barely able to get around. He showed his visitor the stump where his right foreleg had once been and the synthetic marvel which had replaced his entire left leg from the hip down – and they talked briefly about land mines and the hells of warfare in a hostile land. Then Meyer took Bolan to the basement in an elevator he'd built himself and showed him some of the fine weapons he'd also built himself, and some he'd modified or rebuilt, and some he'd merely picked up from one place or another.

He sold a lot of stuff to the Panthers, he explained, also to various fascist and militant leftist groups, and even a couple of cops did business there from time to time.

Meyer's cynical smile told Bolan as much as his words did, and Bolan understood that smile. He had seen it on a lot of warriors who'd left parts of their bodies on the battlefields.

This particular smile told Bolan that a munitions maker did not take sides . . . he was pure like Rachel Silver and just did his thing building destruction for whatever damn fools wanted to come along and set it loose upon the world. Yeah, and Bolan was one of those pure fools who came along. It seemed like a lousy way to run a world, but this was no time for Bolan to go into *that* again. He'd searched his soul so many times it was getting raw. Like God, Bolan did not propose – he merely disposed. He made his selections from Meyer's arsenal and paid the man from his rapidly dwindling war chest, adding an extra fifty for special delivery to a midtown parcel depot.

While returning to the surface in the elevator, Bolan elicited the information that a guy could pick up some action in the rear of a barber shop just around the corner – anything from lottery to craps and horses – he could even get contact numbers for business girls, if Bolan was so inclined, but they would run from fifty to a hundred per wallop. Meyer also assured him that the place was secure against busts, a point which Bolan seemed very concerned with. Sure, the joint enjoyed the protection of one Freddie Gambella. Yes, Meyer had met Gambella once – big in the rackets, but a nice guy after all. No, Meyer had never supplied arms for Gambella. He understood that the mob had their own sources, legit ones – they couldn't be bothered with a small business man like William Meyer.

Bolan could. There were times when Bolan simply had to believe in fate. The Executioner left the small businessman and went directly to the 'protected' back room just around the corner.

He found quite an operation going there. The 'back room' was four times larger than the shop itself. There were slots, card and crap tables, football pools galore, and bootleg lottery and offtrack racing stalls in direct competition with the State of New York. Bolan drifted through and counted more than a dozen obvious employees – how many not-so-obvious

53

ones would be anybody's guess. He located the inevitable back-room-behind-the-back-room where all the goodies would be kept, the door to which was being protected by two guys in honest to God security-guard uniforms.

It was simply too much to pass up. Bolan had not dipped into the Mafia's wealth since Los Angeles, and the war chest was about flattened. He debated the advisability of pulling a soft recon first and returning later with a battle plan, then decided that he would probably do just as well to simply play it by ear and dive right in. The recent skirmish in the Bronx would no doubt have Gambella presently somewhat off balance, and Bolan would probably find no better time for a knockover than right now.

He ran a hand inside his jacket and fingered the outline of the shoulder wound. It felt fine. Okay Freddie, stand by for a ram.

Bolan composed his face into a scowl and marched right at the door to the goody chamber. One of the uniformed guards moved uncertainly to one side, no more than half a step but it was all Bolan had been looking for. He elbowed the guy and growled, 'Come on, come on.'

His hand was on the door and the guards were exchanging uneasy looks with each other when the one who had yielded came out with a confused challenge. 'Who are – I don't seem to – you gotta have an ID to get in there.'

'Aw shit,' Bolan said, his voice dripping with disgust. 'You fuckin' clowns better learn what's what or you'll have Freddie's ID stamp all over your ass.' He fixed the worried one with a cold stare. 'Are you gonna push that button or aren't you?'

The guard's eyes wavered and his hand fumbled to the wall behind him. In a very dry voice he said, 'Mr. uh . . .'

Bolan snapped, 'Mr. Lambretta, and you better never have to ask again.'

'Yes sir, Mr. Lambretta, I'll remember that.' The guard's finger found the button and punched out a code. Seconds later a buzzer sounded on the door and the guard pushed it open and held it wide for Bolan's entry. 'Sorry about the foul-up, Mr. Lambretta. Go right in.'

Bolan growled, 'Forget it,' and went right in.

It was a typical setup. A vault and several desks with adding machines and calculators behind a wire fence, a short counter with a mixed assortment of men and women, some old and some young, perched on stools counting money and feeding coins into roller machines. Two more uniformed guards, one at the door through which Bolan had just entered, another at a door to the rear – alleyway, Bolan guessed – holding burpguns, no less.

Typical but big – it was one hell of a big operation. Bolan read *central station* all over the place. It was a clearing house and bank for street runners. This joint was not just being *protected* by Gambella. Bolan was betting his life that it was owned lock, stock, and barrel by the mob. His eyes found the controller with no difficulty whatever – a harried-looking little man with white hair and gold-rimmed glasses.

Bolan slapped the front door guard on the rump as he strolled past and went directly to the wire cage and caught whitehair's eye and summoned him with a crooking finger. The little man came over and peered at Bolan through the wire mesh, the eyes inquisitive and wondering where he'd seen Bolan before.

Bolan did not give him much time to wonder. In a voice low-pitched and edged with urgency, he told whitehair, 'Don't panic now. I'm Lambretta, Central Precinct. Don't worry. Freddie's on his way over.'

The guy blinked his eyes and grunted, 'Huh?'

'I said don't worry.'

'I don't know what you're talking about,' the controller told him, his breathing staggering a bit. 'Why is Mr. Gambella coming over?'

'Didn't you get the . . . ? Well for Christ's sake!' Bolan's eyes rolled and he leaned closer to the wire mesh and dropped his voice even lower. 'I thought *Freddie* was going to . . . never mind. There's a raid called. Three o'clock. Feds and everybody, the full bit. You're supposed to be getting the stuff out of here. You telling me you haven't done anything yet?'

Whitehair's lips firmed up and he whirled about without a word and began moving quickly among his book-keepers and clerks. Things began happening, quickly and quietly. Ledgers and tapes began disappearing into canvas pouches. A youngish man with a deformed spine spun the wheel in the vault, opened the door, and stepped inside. Bolan heard a woman clerk call the whitehaired one 'Mr. Feldman' and a big brawny guy started tossing canvas satchels in a pile on the floor.

Feldman stepped back to the mesh fence and told Bolan, 'Yes, we're taking care of it. What about out front?'

Bolan shook his head and turned a thumb toward the floor. 'We're letting them have the front.'

The controller nodded his head in understanding. His face fell into sorrowing lines and he confided to Bolan, 'All these years with Mr. Gambella and this is my first bust.'

'Well, there's a first time for everything,' Bolan philosophized. 'These goddam feds are running wild.'

'It's a damn shame,' Feldman said, and spun around and went into the vault.

Feldman had no idea, Bolan was thinking, how big a shame it was. The pace was picking up, clerks dashing about in excitement, slamming things about in an ever-rising noise level. The guards were beginning to fidget and obviously wonder what the hell was coming off. Bolan walked down to the one at the rear door and asked him, 'Is the truck here?'

'What truck?' the guy asked, his eyebrows gathering into a perplexed scowl.

Bolan threw up his hands in a resigned gesture and he cried, 'Well kiss my ass! Nobody sent for the *truck*?'

The guard shifted his weight from one foot to the other as he replied, 'If you mean the armored car, it ain't due 'til five o'clock.'

'I know when it's *due*!' Bolan yelled 'We gott a get this stuff outta here *now*! You get your ass out there and *get* something!'

The guard gawked at him with rising bewilderment, then he threw a pleading look toward the wire fence. Feldman, drawn by Bolan's yelling, was coming through the gate with a worried face. The guard asked him, 'What's this guy talking about?'

'We have an emergency, Harry,' the controller told him. 'Have to move everything out, and quick Get us some transportation. We'll need ... oh hell, we'll need several cars or a fairsize van. You'd better see what you can do.'

'Well how much time've I got?' the bewildered Harry wanted to know.

'You've got about ten damned minutes!' Bolan snarled. 'You better get your ass in gear!'

The other guard had come down to join the discussion. Harry thrust his burpgun at him and muttered, 'Shit, I'm a security man, not no goddam transportation expert. Awright, somebody let me out.'

Feldman went back behind the cage and pressed the door release. The buzzer squawked and Harry stepped into the alleyway muttering to himself. The other guard was standing there with a dumb look and a burpgun under each arm. Bolan took one of them, saying, 'Here, give me th' damn thing. Listen, you may as well go out there too. Don't let anyone get curious and start hanging around.'

The guard looked to the controller for an okay. Feldman nodded his head and again operated the doorlock. The guy went out, greatly perturbed and fiddling with the visor of his cap.

The man with the crooked spine came out of the vault pushing a wheeled cart bearing neatly wrapped packages.

Bolan stepped in through the open gate and placed the burpgun on the counter as the crippled man was reporting progress. 'These are the tabulated receipts through noon today, Mr. Feldman. We'll have the balance in about five minutes. We're just going to sack it, if that's all right.'

The controller jerked his head in a quick okay. 'And leave the coin,' he commanded.

Bolan picked up one of the packages from the cart and was looking it over. It was a five-grand bundle. Yes, this was definitely a central station. There were at least fifty of those packets on the cart. And someone had said that legalized betting in New York would put the mob on to hard times.

Bolan grabbed a canvas satchel off the floor and began stuffing it with five-grand packages. Feldman watched him for a moment, then said, 'Why don't we just leave it on the cart? If Harry gets a van . . .'

Bolan replied, 'And suppose he can't? You just want to toss these packages loose into the seat of a car?' He zipped the bag shut and threw it at the rear door, twenty-five thousand dollars worth, then grabbed another.

Feldman stood there through a brief moment of indecision, then he too began transferring the packets into a bag. Bolan completed his second baggy job and gave it a toss, then told the controller, 'Hey listen, I'm going to go out there and see what that clown is doing.'

Feldman nodded his head agreeably, obviously happy to lose 'Lambretta's' company. Bolan picked up the burpgun and walked to the door, then turned to stare at the white-haired man. 'The fuckin' door,' he growled.

The controller grimaced and moved impatiently to send the unlock signal to the door mechanism, then turned away with an unhappy scowl. Bolan pulled the door open, kicked a money bag outside, quietly dropped a marksman's medal to the floor, and went out. The door clicked behind him and he told the waiting guard, 'Watch that satchel, it's got twenty-five thou in it,' then he walked quickly to the end of the alley,

58

a matter of twenty-odd steps, peered into the street briefly and immediately returned to the doorway.

He told the guard, 'Okay, you keep your eyes peeled. Here, take this damn gun.' He shoved the burpgun into the guy's hand, picked up the satchel of money, and walked away.

Bolan did not look back as he made the turn on to the street. He was afraid to. The corners of his mouth were beginning to twitch out of control, and he might burst out laughing if he had to look at that guard's face one more time.

The Executioner could not feel a bit bad about stealing from the mob, and he could think of no one he would rather have contribute to his war chest than Freddie Gambella.

Somebody was going to be catching a lot of hell, of course, but Bolan would save his sympathy for people who deserved it. That den of thieves back there would get everything they had coming to them. As for Gambella, if he thought *this* hurt then he'd better wait awhile.

The tall man with the canvas satchel went on unhurriedly along the quiet street and stepped aboard a downtown bus, and the corners of his mouth were still twitching, and he was wondering if Harry would ever come back with those wheels.

Bolan dropped into a seat across from an elderly black lady, and he allowed himself to break down and laugh a little. The lady was darting curious glances his way, but Bolan didn't mind. A pure fool had engaged the enemy in an act of pure war, and he'd exited laughing. Yeah, it was a hell of a way to run a world. But it would have to do until something better came along. Pure love, maybe. Yeah, and Bolan found himself thinking about Rachel Silver. Yeah. Pure love.

CHAPTER SIX

FRIENDS

FREDDIE GAMBELLA was seated casually in the big swivel chair, a telephone held to the side of his head by a softly manicured hand, when Sam the Bomber pushed hesitantly into the panelled library and made his way softly across the cushioned floor. Sam never had felt overly comfortable in this room – maybe it was the books that made him feel so depressed – and he was feeling particularly out of sorts on this visit.

Gambella threw his visitor a flash of the eyes that told him to have a seat, and he growled softly into the telephone, 'He traded a *what* for it?'

Sam sat down and watched the muscles bunching and un-bunching in the *Capo's* jaw, then he studied his own hands and picked nervously at the bandaids on his fingers. Sam always hated to come in and find Freddie on the goddam telephone, Jesus he hated just sitting there watching and listening and wondering when his turn would come.

'Well I guess I just can't figure it,' Freddie was saying. 'Were they all hypnotized? You mean he just walks in there and passes himself off as a made cop and starts giving orders and they all just snapped shit?'

The first gaze rested on Sam the Bomber as the receiver rattled a longwinded response, then Freddie cut in on it. 'Stop,' he commanded in a thick voice. 'Don't tell me any more about it. I don't want to know. I don't want to hear such dumb . . . I just don't understand Feldman, and I don't want to. All these years and he – listen, we got telephones, right? You just pick up the little gadget and you tap out a number, right? And you get instant advice, right? I want to know why Feldman wasn't looking for some instant advice. You get me, Tommy?'

That would be Tommy Doctor, Sam was thinking. And he was wondering what the doctor had done to get on the carpet this way, Freddie didn't usually talk this way to his people. All that anger was usually buried in a quiet manner and a gentle tone, only you always knew it was there *when* it was there — Freddie had a way of letting you know without getting himself all worked up on the outside. Sam just hoped that what the boss was saying to Tommy Doctor had nothing at all to do with Sam Chianti. And then Sam's heart lurched as the next words came — yeah, they sure had *something* to do with him.

'Now you listen to me, Tommy. I want Bolan, and I don't want no *excuses*, I want the *man*. You put the boys in cars, and you put them walking the streets. You put boys sitting on their asses in bars and cafes, and you put boys everywhere in this town. I want boys in subway stations, air terminals, bus and train depots. I want our cabs alerted, and I want every street worker, every union hall, every precinct station, every committee, every club, every joint, I want everybody in this town looking for Bolan.' Freddie's eyes were starting to bulge and he was running out of breath. A bad sign. 'And Tommy ... don't you talk to me again until you're telling me that you've *got* Bolan. Have I made myself clear?'

The receiver made one or two faint sounds and Freddie said, 'Just don't forget it,' and he hung up and turned his undiluted attention to his lifelong friend, Sam the Bomber.

'I guess you got the most of that,' Fred told Sam.

Chianti nodded his head miserably and fingered a bandaid at his chin. 'Yes, and I understand exactly how you feel, Freddie.'

'You couldn't have the merest notion of how I feel, Sam,'

the *Capo* told him. 'Bolan just knocked over my Harlem bank.'

Chianti sucked in his breath and his eyes began to grow. 'Well that . . .! How the hell did he do that!'

Gambella raised both palms, then turned them over and let them fall to the desk 'He just walks in, trades Feldman a marksman's medal for a bag worth twenty-five thou, and he just walks out.'

Sam the Bomber's eyes were flitting rapidly from Freddie's eyes to Freddie's hands, big manicured hams trying to claw something off the desk that wasn't there.

He said, 'Listen Freddie. You'n me have been friends for a long time, and I don't feel like I'm overstepping my place by mentioning that. The thing is, I wouldn't bullshit you. Not you, not ever. Everything I got in the world I owe you, and I realize that. Listen, this Bolan boy is pure poison. That boy is as dangerous as a bag of snakes with a rip in the side, and you know it the minute he comes up and looks at you. What I'm saying is this, don't hold it too tight against Feldman and those boys in Harlem. This Bolan has a way about him. Whatever he done to get that money, you can bet your ass he did it like a real pro. I mean, he—'

'I know what you mean, Sammy,' Gambella broke in with a tired sigh. He was looking at the adhesives on Chianti's hands and face. 'From the broken glass, eh?' he commented in a sympathetic tone.

Sam said, 'Yeah, and I got off lucky. Oh and I – what I really came in to tell you is this – we dumped the car and all in Brooklyn, and I guess I'm clean on that. We left it where they'd be found, so I guess they can get a decent burial. Jesus I'm glad I didn't have to explain all that to a bunch of unfriendly cops.' He touched the facial bandaids and added, 'So I come out with just a few scratches. I figure I got off lucky.'

'So did I,' Gambella replied heavily. 'He knocked me over for only twenty-five thou. He could have had a quarter mil just as easy, from what I hear. Had 'em all running around gathering it up for him. Even that dumbass guard out trying to steal a truck to haul it away with.'

Sam shook his head and said, 'Well I guess he just wanted to prove something. That's what I figured, over in the Bronx. He didn't come in after me. I guess he never meant to all the time.'

'Yeah, he proved something,' Gambella said thoughtfully. 'Look – I'm not afraid of this boy, Sammy, but I'm worried about him. I mean, he's a damn pest and I want him out of my hair. We have this big thing coming up, and I don't want this guy roaring around town and lousing it up. You know what I mean.'

'Yeah, I know,' Sam the Bomber replied. 'You're right, the guy is a damn pest. He needs to get swatted, and good, I'm not afraid of him, either. I just wish I could get a long enough look at him to swat him. I didn't even see him out there today. Just suddenly *wham*, and all hell is breaking loose.'

Sam shivered, then chuckled self-consciously. 'I was lying. I'm scared of this boy, Freddie. Listen, there's no bullshitting between old friends. This boy scares the pee outta me. But that don't mean I'm going to turn tail and run from him. I'll swat that boy, Freddie, if I get just half a chance.'

'I know you will, Sammy,' the boss told him in a quiet voice.

'Tommy Doctor is one damned good engineer. If anybody can run a find on Bolan, it's him.'

'College boys,' Gambella sneered derisively.

'Well college boys ain't like they used to be, Sam. They got a lotta starch in their ass nowadays.'

Gambella's eyes were focused on the window in a blank stare. Quietly, he said, 'You know, I wish Bolan had waited just two months. If he louses up this big thing we got going . . .'

He sighed and gave his friend a tired smile. 'You know it was no more'n a couple of weeks ago I voted to give Bolan this peace offer. I guess he spit on that. And now here he is in my town and raising hell here. I got to go to a special meeting tonight, over this very thing. The other four are nervouser than I am, and I guess with good reason. They got more tied up in it, I mean more at stake. Why didn't Bolan just wait a couple more months? Now he's come here looking for a war, and I guess we got to give him one. But I just wish . . .'

After a quiet moment, Chianti suggested, 'Maybe he's just passing through, Freddie. Maybe he wanted that twenty-five thou to just blow with.'

'Naw,' Gambella replied, sighing. 'He's starting out just like always. With that famous 1-2-3 of his. Just look at it, Sam. He hits you over in the Bronx at what? – one o'clock? – a quarter 'til? – then he pops up in Harlem at a little after two and knocks over my bank. So he'll be hitting again, pretty soon, just hold your breath and wait, it'll come. The number three punch, he may already be throwing it. I just wish I knew where.'

'Tommy Doctor will—'

'*Bull*shit Tommy Doctor!' the *Capo* yelled.

Chianti jumped and stiffened in his chair. Boy, this was getting under Freddie's skin in the worst . . .

'Don't tell me no more Tommy Doctor!' Gambella said coldly, regaining outward control, but the street language filtering back told Sam that the surface calm only thinly covered a seething storm just below. 'Listen, Sam, what are friends for? Huh?'

Chianti fidgeted and puffed out his throat and said thickly, 'No greater love has a man but he will put it down for his friend, Freddie. And that's me, you know that.'

'Exactly,' the *Capo* said.

'Well, uh . . .'

'Just don't tell me no more Tommy Doctors. You get out on those streets, Sam. You put it on the pavement for me and thee.'

64

Sam the Bomber came awkwardly out of the chair and stood there for a moment, his eyes flicking sickly from item to item on the *Capo's* desk. He muttered, 'I been off the streets a long time, Freddie.'

'*Too* long,' the *Capo* said.

'Uh, yeah, I guess so. I guess I'm pretty rusty. I guess I better go see what I can do about that.'

'I guess so, Sam.'

Chianti whirled away and went back across the spongy floor, knowing now why he hated to come in there, knowing the spongy floor was actually a bed of quicksand, not thick carpeting; quicksand that drags a guy down to his choking, floundering doom, just like some *friendships* could.

He paused at the doorway and turned a pained face upon his friend the *Capo* and quietly told him, 'See you, Fred.'

'Give regards to Theresa.'

'Yeah,' Sam the Bomber murmured, and went back out to the streets where he had started. And where, he guessed, he would finish.

CHAPTER SEVEN

SPECIES

It was just past five o'clock, it was dark and a light snowfall was beginning, and Bolan's busy day was barely under-way.

He had gone from Harlem to the East Village where he took on an entire new wardrobe, from buckskin trousers and vest to high moccasins and campaign hat. He also picked up a headband and numerous strings of beads, freak glasses with purple lenses, and a leather hip pouch. Then he took another tip from his invaluable little poop book and found a place in the old Jewish community of the lower East Side where a guy could buy wheels fully equipped with license and all the legalties, on a moment's notice and without red tape, pro-vided he had the ready cash.

Bolan had the cash, and he drove away in a four year old VW micro-bus in excellent condition with daisies painted across the outer surfaces.

From there he proceeded directly to the midtown parcel service and picked up his shipment from William Meyer & Company, and now he was in the rush hour crush at the Queens-Midtown Tunnel. An airport bus from the East Side Terminal, jockeying for position into the tunnel approach, did its best to cancel out Bolan's proudest purchase of the day, but Bolan hit his brakes, skidded into an adjacent lane, stood a glistening Caddy on its nose there, and listened to a traffic cop yell at him for at least thirty seconds until the line lurched forward and he eased out of earshot. And then he was into the tube and wondering why any sane person would go through all this twice a day every day of his life. Bolan would take the battlefield, thanks, and leave the traffic ulcers to those who worked for them.

Things moved swiftly in the underground tube and he was approaching the toll gate in Queens before he could find his change. He took some more berating while he dug for it, and then he was off and running along the suicide trail toward Long Island.

The VW was slow on the takeoff, but once she got fully wound-up Bolan was hanging in there with the best of them, and the ugly duckling of the auto world turned out to be a pretty sweet little roadrunner, after all.

Bolan knew precisely where he was going, though he had never been there before — the place was no more to him than a spot on a map and a flag in his memory of many whispered conversations. The mob called the joint *Stoney Lodge*. It was a hardsite, a home away from home for rankholders in the organization and a place where a guy could relax, let go of the cares of the streets and forget territorial competitions. Women, it was said, were absolutely taboo and even the waiters and bartenders wore gunleather. There were grassy fields where a guy could go out and shoot a tethered pheasant, or try his luck chasing down a fenced deer in a jeep. The chef had once been a noted Manhattan restauranteur, or so the story went, and the wine cellar had all the best years of France, Italy, and California.

The five bosses of New York held many of their business councils there and, if the stories Bolan had heard were true, some of the best known politicians in the East had been wined and dined at one time or another at Stoney Lodge. As a hardsite, it boasted a formidable palace guard throughout a twenty-four hour day, and it was regarded as an impregnable fortress. Or so the stories went. Yeah, Bolan knew precisely where he was headed.

He left the Long Island Expressway at Jericho, climbed northward past East Norwich and Oyster Bay, then he was navigating by the seat of his pants and the VW's odometer, carefully marking the tenths of miles between one obscure little road and the next, and picking his way along the inlets and points of Long Island Sound.

It was seven o'clock when he located his target and began a soft recon of the area on foot. The snow was just beginning to come in light flurries out here. It was melting as it hit and the earth underfoot was becoming a bit tacky. The night had a friendly blackness, though, and Bolan had no weather complaints.

A six-foot high brick wall with barbed wire strung along the top separated the site from the rest of the world. Floodlights were emplaced at intervals of about every fifty feet. Bolan remained clear of the lights and walked off one entire side of the plot, and from this he computed the total area behind that fencing at about ten acres. Then he backed off and found a high point of ground from which to make a binocular survey of the interior grounds. The place was lit up like Christmas, and there was little difficulty in picking out the salient features.

The main building was a three story job of stone and heavy timber with porches jutting out here and there at all three levels. A long veranda traversed one entire side at ground level, and Bolan found hints of a larger patio area to the rear. There would be a pool back there, he surmised, and all the gaudy pleasures that normally accompanied the good life. Several smaller buildings were clustered about the primary structure, and the entire building complex was set in about one hundred yards from the front gate. A well-lighted macadam road ran straight as an arrow from the gate to the lodge area, then looped about a good-size parking area and angled off somewhere into the darkness.

Bolan had kept his mind loose as to his reasons for trekking out here. He had known about the joint, he had wanted to see it, and perhaps in the depths of his mind somewhere had been a vague plan to go out there and level the joint, smash it to powder, kill everything that moved, and show the Five Families that there was no such place as an impregnable fortress of safety where they could R and R things up. But there could be no practical value to such a hit – not unless he could chance upon a gathering of the clans. Even so, as purely a mission of psychological warfare it would be a worthwhile operation if he could pull it off properly. But his surveillance was suggesting to him that he could not. There was no way of knowing the defenses until a guy actually got down in there, and then an awful truth might come.

Bolan pondered the situation and finally decided firmly against a hard hit. There were too many variables, too many unknowns, and he was not exactly in the best form. A *soft probe*, though, as long as he was out here, might be entirely in order. He went back to his bus, wrapped himself in a black poncho, and returned to the observation point. There he stayed for one hour, watching the windows of the big house, occasionally turning the binoculars on to the grounds and along the wall, watching for some activity about the gatehouse. He found no activity anywhere, except for an occasional shadow moving across a lighted window in the lodge, and once he thought he glimpsed something moving through a patch of light on the grounds.

The time was shortly past eight o'clock when Bolan returned to the VW the second time and stripped down to his midnight combat suit. It was a thermal outfit and would provide protection from the cold if he did not stay too long in one spot. As other items of protection, he kept the Beretta and the shoulder rig and added a web belt with ammo packets to his waist. A light chatter gun from the Meyer arsenal went around his neck and he clipped a pair of fragmentation grenades to the web belt.

Several minutes later the Executioner was over the wall and moving silently on a parallel course with the macadam road. The ground was smooth like a golf green and trying to freeze, and the snow was coming a bit thicker but still not laying on the ground. Soon it would begin to accumulate. He knew that he would have to conclude his probe with all speed and get the hell out before he started making tracks about that hardsite.

Bolan was about halfway to the building complex when he thought he heard something moving toward him through the darkness. He dropped to one knee and froze, the beretta up and ready, eyes straining ahead to pierce the night and hopefully to get that initial advantage of first glimpse.

The opponent of the moment, however, had a much greater perceptual range and sense development far surpassing the mere human faculties of Mack Bolan. Almost. Bolan heard the thing snorting and sensed the rush of the attack, and he went over on his side just as the foe loomed out of the blackness, lips curled back and teeth gleaming in a low-pitched snarl, a charging German Shepherd in a killing mood, a black devil of the night, and Bolan nearly tore his head off with two quick phuts of the Beretta.

Bolan was silently damning himself for not knowing better, for failing to understand the total absence of human activity on those grounds. He was in a no-man's-land ruled by killer canines – and the big question now was how many more of them were about. He got an immediate partial answer as another item of snarling death came in from the other flank. The Beretta dropped this one in mid-leap and one of the fangs grazed Bolan's gun hand as the furry ball hit the ground and slid past him.

There was something particularly immoral about this kind of a fight, something that jangled at Bolan and ruffled him deepdown where he lived. He crouched there, breathing hard and waiting for the next one, and the realization came on him stronger than ever before that man was just another kind of animal, a beast of prey that devoured its victims' flesh, killing to live, and ofttimes living to kill. And in moments of stress such as this, he reverted back to type and became more animal than man.

Bolan felt a terrible kinship with those dead beasts lying there, and in a sudden flash of insight he understood beasts like Sam the Bomber and Freddie Gambella. They had been brutalized by forces they did not comprehend, the same as those German Shepherds. And they reverted to type, the same as those Shepherds had done.

And what about Mack Bolan? Hadn't he become brutalized as well? Yes. Sure he had. But that realization did not change anything. The whole thing was a point of survival, and every man had to survive his own way. Brutalized men survived through brutality, or failed through it. If another Shepherd came, Bolan would kill him – and if a *Mafioso* came, Bolan would kill him too.

Suppose he had tried to *reason* with those devil dogs that came on him from the blackness of night? Who would be lying there, torn and dead, a survival failure? Bolan knew who, and he knew that a guy would get the same results trying to reason with a *Mafioso*. You didn't reason with brutes, you simply killed them. Many people had tried to co-exist with the Mafia, and the Mafia had left them torn and bleeding. Well – Bolan had his own way of surviving, and it was *their* way, and the main difference between them lay in Bolan's ability to use it faster and better. He knew that he would remain alive only so long as that difference existed.

Now he had decided that there were no more dogs, or they would have been along by now. He went on, warily continued the soft probe, and he saw many interesting things which went into his mental file.

Then he withdrew, took the dead dogs with him and buried them beside the VW, and laid his plans for another day as he made the long drive back to Manhattan.

He knew that hardsite now, he knew its defenses and its weaknesses, and he knew how to grind it to powder. And one day very soon he would do just that.

CHAPTER EIGHT

LOVERS

THE hour was late and the roads were practically deserted in a rapidly developing snowstorm. On a sudden impulse, Bolan took the interchange into the Cross Island Expressway for a swing through the Bronx. It was about as good a way as any to get to Manhattan, at this late hour, and Bolan found himself being drawn back to the neighborhood of Sam the Bomber. He felt curiously frustrated and at loose ends with himself, as though the day somehow should not be allowed to end on the note he'd taken with him from Stoney Lodge. Sam the Bomber represented an item of unfinished business, a loose end that needed tucking in.

Bolan cruised past the house that Human Engineering had restored and saw nothing but a faint nightlight to the rear, then he drove on into the next block and found a place to leave the VW. The snowflakes were wet and bloated and being pushed by a respectable wind, yet Bolan went into it with nothing to keep him warm but the Beretta and the thermal suit.

New glass had replaced the mess of the earlier hit; all was still and dead at the front of the house. Bolan went on around the side and into drifting snow and silence and darkness, reaching the rear just as a heavy car came whining slowly up the alley, wheels spinning with too much power versus too little traction. Headlamps arced across and momentarily illuminated the rear of Chianti's house, then abruptly disappeared as the car wheeled into a garage. Bolan moved swiftly across the open area and reached the corner of the garage jut as the engine was silenced.

A door slammed, then another, and a muffled voice said something in an impatient tone. A light went on inside the garage and a roller-door slid to a close, then a floodlight came on and illuminated the area between the garage and the house. Bolan pressed into the shadows and waited.

Another rumble of voices, a deep male basso voicing a complaint about the weather and having to drive in it, another one saying something with regards to what had to be expected at this time of year. Then a side door opened and a big guy in a trench coat emerged, stepping directly in front of Bolan. The butt of the Beretta slammed into the base of the big guy's skull and he pitched forward into the snow with a soft grunt.

Sam the Bomber apeared in the open doorway. He said, 'Dammit, Al, I *told* you to watch your . . .' And then he saw Bolan, and the wicked black Beretta, and he said, inanely, 'Oh hell, I thought he slipped.'

Bolan told him, 'You both slipped, Sam.'

Then a third person stepped into the light and looked Bolan over in a cool appraisal, and Bolan knew an impulse to turn around and walk away from there. She was an older version of Valentina, the girl he had loved and left in Pittsfield so many lifetimes ago, and she was giving him that same disapproving look which Val had used on him from time to time.

She saw the Beretta, of course, and there was little doubt that she knew who Bolan was and why he was there. But she cooled it, and told him in a chatty tone, 'Such a night to be out, and you in little more than underwear. I told Sam we could go some other night, Thursday maybe, but you would have thought tonight was the last chance he would ever have. So we drove clear to Connecticut just to see the children, and in this weather, and we just saw them Sunday.'

She was watching Bolan's face, and he had to look away from those eyes; he knew what she was telling him, and he did not wish to offer her any false comfort.

Chianti told her, 'Go on in the house, Theresa.'

She was maybe forty, and way out of Sam's class if Bolan was any judge. But then, Val had been out of Bolan's class, too – yet she had prayed over him and wept over him and begged him to just let her love him. Bolan was wondering if Theresa prayed and wept over her Sam.

She was looking right past the Beretta and into Bolan's eyes as she told her husband, 'Why don't you ask your friend in out of the snow and I'll put on some coffee.'

Chianti said, 'Yeah, that's a good idea, Theresa. You go put on the coffee. We'll be along in a minute.'

Bolan had not spoken since that first terse announcement to Sam the Bomber. He was looking at Theresa Chianti but he was seeing and thinking of Valentina, dear tender Val with the guts of a Viking and the heart of an angel – and he had not thought of her for a long time, *would not* think of her. He did not want to think of Sam the Bomber's wife either. This was a side of the wars he had always diligently avoided; Bolan did not like to think of weeping widows.

Now he spoke, and he told the composed little woman, 'It's a good night for coffee, Mrs. Chianti.'

Her eyes sparkled and she threw a quick glance at her husband, a glance that she must have known might have to last her a lifetime, and she smiled at Bolan and her gaze lingered for a moment on the fallen bodyguard, and then she went toward the house.

Sam murmured, 'Hold it just a minute, huh Bolan? Until she gets inside.'

Bolan held it. He said, 'I'm sorry about the lady, Sam.'

The doomed man sighed and replied, 'Me too. Uh, I don't guess you'd like to take me somewheres else for it. I mean, I'd sure rather Theresa didn't have to see it.'

The snow was swirling between them in sticky gobs and

74

clustering about Sam's face and melting and running down in rivulets. The Beretta and Bolan's gun hand were beginning to show an accumulation also, but that hand had not wavered.

Now the black blaster waggled ever so faintly and Bolan said, 'Are you packing, Sam?'

Chianti nodded his head. 'In my belt, left side.'

'So use two fingers of your left hand and get rid of it.'

The *Mafioso's* face showed that he thought his request was to be granted. He did as he was told, dropping a snub-nosed .38 into the snow at his feet.

The weather was not bothering the Executioner, but a spreading coldness was centering in his chest, deep inside. He told the contractor's contractor. 'You need to retire Sam.'

'I been thinking about that,' came the somber reply.

The woman had reached the house. A light came on, in what was obviously the kitchen, and Bolan could see her standing there at the window, hands clasped in front of her. He told Chianti, 'If I were you, I'd stop thinking about it, and I'd do it.'

'If I had a chance, Bolan, I think I would,' Chianti replied in a voice already dead.

Bolan's words were as cold as that spot in his chest as he told the contractor, 'You've got that chance, Sam. But only one. After tonight, your chances are all used up. So go get some coffee and think about it. Go on.'

It took a couple of seconds for the message to reach the *Mafioso*. He stared at Bolan unbelievingly, then asked, 'You mean it?'

Bolan said, 'For *her* Sam. Not for you. For *her*, one time only.'

Chianti lurched about and staggered toward the house, not looking back once until he reached the top of the steps. Then he threw Bolan a dazed glance and hurried inside. Through the window, Bolan saw the woman throw herself around her husband's neck, and then Bolan got away from there.

Yeah, one time only for love was not asking too much. Bolan just hoped he would not have cause to regret it. Somehow, though, it seemed that he had found a good note with which to close the day.

To state it in Rachel Silver's language, something had sparked between a German Shepherd and a man known as *the Executioner*, and the man had flung that spark back into the beast's face. There *was* a difference. There had to be. Otherwise, survival was not even worth it.

Bolan was wearing his buckskins and purple glasses when he pulled into the garage at the East Side apartment building. The attendant gave the daisied VW a distasteful once-over and told the Executioner, 'This is a private garage.'

Bolan said, 'Don't lay that on me, man. The Lindley chick wants me to pick up some stuff.'

'At one'clock in the morning?'

Bolan shrugged. 'Better late than never, man. Whatsa matter, you got house rules here, curfew or something?'

The guys eyes wavered. He asked, 'Who did you say?'

'Lindley,' Bolan replied boredly. He squinted at an open notebook lying on the seat beside him and added, 'Eleven-G, it says here.'

The attendant nodded and picked up a house phone.

Bolan suggested, 'Tell her it's the Man from Blood.'

The guy gave him a hard look. Bolan chuckled and told him, 'That's the name of the service, dad. *You* change it, I can't.'

The garage attendant completed the call, spoke briefly into the phone, and told Bolan, 'Okay. Park over there at the service dock. And keep the noise down, it's a little late for commercial calls.'

A minute-and-a-half later Bolan was pushing the button

76

outside the Lindley-Clifford-Silver apartment. Lindley responded, her face a study in perplexed anxiety. She wore a transparent negligee and little else, and the initial reaction to the hippy-type at the door was a confused one.

Then Bolan smiled and pulled off the freak glasses. She grabbed him and pulled him inside and closed the door, all in the space of one muffled little yelp. She gasped, 'We had you dead!'

Bolan said, 'Not quite. I'm only staying a minute – just wanted to check you out.'

'Well gee thanks! You could have called or left a message or something, you know!' She was building up a head of outraged steam. 'I mean, we didn't nurse you night and day just to ho-hum you out of our lives with no idea whatever of what had become of . . .'

She ran out of breath and steam at the same time and melted against him, arms encircling his neck and pressing into a close embrace. Bolan rubbed her spine and patted her hip and told her, 'You're right, I should have checked back sooner.'

'I wish you had,' Paula murmured. She pushed away from him and nervously massaged her forehead, 'Evie has been so shook up . . . she ran out of here about eight o'clock to look for you . . . and she isn't back yet.'

Bolan said, 'That was a dumb—'

'She had good reason!' Paula cried, flaring up again.

He was showing her a baffled frown. 'You'd better give me all of it.'

She said, 'Well it begins with a bloodstained foyer and an empty apartment. Obviously there had been a fight here, of some sort. It looked as though they had caught up with you, and took you away. We knew it couldn't have been the police, or they would have been here waiting for us. Then Evie began having hysterics all over the place. She thought she was responsible. You've noticed, I'm sure, that Evie talks

77

a lot. It seems that she had let something slip about you staying here, and she—'

Bolan interrupted with a taut, 'Who'd she slip it to?'

Paula tossed her head nervously and replied, 'She's been running around with this political action group, a young lib movement. She had lunch with a couple of the boys today. They've been having a lot of trouble lately with the hardhat faction, and the boys were discussing this. So Evie bubbled out with the information that she had just the man to take care of that problem. One thing led to another and she was swearing them to secrecy and telling them ... all about ... *you*.'

Bolan sighed and said, 'Damn, this could be dangerous, Paula. Not for me so much as for you girls.'

'Well, at any rate, Evie left here at eight o'clock to touch base with the lib group and to find out just how far the story had gone. And I'm getting worried ... I can't reach any of them by telephone ... and, well, she's been gone five hours.'

'And Rachel?'

'Rachel has been meditating ever since we discovered the bloodstains.'

Bolan made a pained face and asked, 'Is it unusual for Evie to be out this late?'

Paula shook her head. 'No, she's a free spirit. But ... well, it was her frame of mind when she left here, and ...' She pulled on a bright smile and said, 'Oh nuts. If I had a dime for every hour I've spent worrying about that dumb bunny, I could branch out. Now, Evie is completely out of my mind. *You* are there. Let me fix you something to eat, and you tell me what you've been up to.' She was moving across the foyer and tugging at Bolan.

He stopped her and told her, 'No, I can't say. I came by to pick up my stuff and let you know I'm okay.'

'So you're checking out,' she said, giving him the sorrowing eye.

He nodded. 'It's time, isn't it.'

78

She sighed. 'I guess it is. You have a place to stay, huh?'

He said, 'Yeah. Little joint near Central Park. Serves my purposes fine. Look, Paula ... I appreciate ... I'll keep in touch, eh.'

'You do that,' she replied soberly.

'Could I, uh, get you to bring my suitcase out here? Tell Rachel, eh, after I've left, tell her I ... hell, you know what to tell her.'

'Yes, I know what to tell her,' Paula said woodenly.

She whirled away in a flash of silk. Bolan watched her cross the big room and thought of how nice it could be for an ordinary guy who didn't have to worry about jeopardizing every life he touched.

Then she was back with the suitcase and walking him to the door.

She dropped the bag to the floor and informed him, 'You're going to kiss me goodbye, mister.'

He did so, and she moulded against him at every possible joining surface. The soft lips held him and dizzied him as warm sweet currents passed through and finally he broke the connection and told her in a ragged whisper, 'That's some crazy therapy,' and then he had the door open and the bag in his hand and he was getting away while he could.

He looked back as he rounded the corner to the elevators, and she was still there in the doorway and he thought *God*, how he'd love to have a normal life.

Downstairs, he made a production out of opening the side door to the micro-bus and rattling the bag around as he stowed it, then he tossed a wave toward the attendant's shack and called over, 'Groove, dad, mission accomplished.'

The guy ignored him. Bolan climbed into the VW and took his time lighting a cigarette before he cranked the engine and turned on his lights and got the windshield wipers in motion, then he eased out the clutch and circled on to the exit ramp.

79

A blur of motion to his left was the only warning, and then Rachel Silver ran into his path and stood there daring him to run her down. She wore a bulky maxi-coat and high-heeled boots, and Bolan was betting nothing else. He hit the brakes and shifted into neutral and crossed his arms atop the steering wheel, and then the door opened and she slid in beside him.

'I'm going with you,' she announced, lips trembling and gasping for breath.

'The hell you are,' he told her.

The attendant had come out of his office and was standing just outside giving Bolan a direct stare.

Rachel said, 'If I'm not, then get ready for the loudest screaming fit of your life.'

Bolan sighed and put the VW into motion. 'I guess you're going with me,' he muttered.

She snuggled toward him and her lips quivered as she told him, 'I saw you dead.'

He eased carefully on to the snowpacked surface of the street and asked her, 'And when was that?'

'About an hour ago. You were lying face down in blood and two men were standing over you and laughing.'

Tightly, Bolan said, 'Wrong guy. As you see, I'm still here.'

'It was a vision,' she explained, shivering violently and scooting closer to him. The coat gaped open momentarily, and, yeah, Bolan won the bet, she wasn't wearing a damned thing beneath it. 'A *vision*,' she repeated, 'not a televised report.'

'Well thanks for the tip,' he said. 'But I get visions like that all the time.'

'Don't joke about it,' she warned him. Both hands went around his arm and she gave it a desperate little squeeze. 'Before you die, Mack Bolan, you're going to give me love.'

Very quietly he told her, 'I think I've already given you

love, Rachel. The only kind I'm able to give. You don't want a dying man, you want a living one. I'm going to circle the block, and I want you to get out, and I want you to go home.'

She shook her head adamantly, the lovely head bobbing about on his shoulder. 'I'll take what you have to give,' she told him.

Bolan's mind had been about eighty per cent on the girl, the other fraction on his driving. Suddenly, though the balance reversed with the heavy end being directed at the snow-blurred rear-vision mirror mounted on the outside doorpost, and on the pair of headlamps that had followed him out of the garage.

He muttered, 'Don't settle for crumbs, Rachel. Go for the full feast.' He made the turn at the corner and watched the headlamps in the mirror do the same thing.

The girl was telling him, 'You may as well save your circling. You're not going to talk me out of it.'

'I might not have to,' he growled as he swung into the next turn and the faithful followers tagged right along.

He shook the girl loose from his gun arm and commanded, 'Get on the floor and stay there.'

'What is it?' she asked calmly.

'Maybe nothing,' he muttered. 'And maybe that vision of yours is coming due. Don't backtalk. Dammit, just get on the floor!'

She dammit got on the floor and she was peering up at him with frightened eyes as he threw the VW into a reckless advance along the slippery street.

'I love you, Mack,' she quietly declared.

He reached for the Beretta and told her, 'I love you too, Rachel.'

And, at the moment anyway, he meant it.

He wanted to love somebody, *any*body, for at least a little while.

His soul was sick to death of survival.

CHAPTER NINE

WORLDS

A LOOMING blob of the city's snow-removal machinery spun around the corner directly in Bolan's path and hogging the intersection, flashing yellow lights trying to tell him what he already knew, but a moment too late. He cranked the wheel and stomped the gas pedal, putting himself into a crabbing slide through the intersection and clearing the behemoth by inches. It whirred on past him and the VW continued in an uncontrolled skid at quarter-broadside, the rear wheels digging futilely at the icy slope along the curbing, front wheels vainly trying to show the way back to the proper track. And then he was really in trouble. The curbing flanged off into a dipping driveway to an underground garage, the VW slipped into it, spun, and came to rest with one rear wheel edged into the curbing at the far side, positioned front-end-out with absolutely nowhere to go.

And moving cautiously past the snow-remover less than a half-block to the rear, came the persistent headlamps of the tail car.

Bolan commanded Rachel to stay put, and leapt out and ran down the street to meet them, intent on keeping the fire-light as far from the VW as possible. The tail car passed beneath the overhead lighting of the intersection, Bolan could see that it was one of the stubby quasi-sportscars of foreign make – hardly typical of mob wheels. At a time like this, though, one did not take chances. He raised the Beretta and rapidfired a line of holes across the top of the windshield in a left to right scan.

The little car immediately went into a spin, the horn sounded briefly, front wheels hit the curbing in a sideways slam and jumped it, and the vehicle came to rest broadside across the sidewalk. Bolan was on the hump of the road, the Beretta at arm's length, sighting down through the swirling snow at pointblank range. A window on the driver's side cracked open and a quavery voice yelled, 'Hey God hold your fire! We're friendly!'

'Come out of there backwards!' Bolan commanded. 'One at a time! Hands on the roof before I see the rest of you!'

The driver came out of there thusly, scrambling in his hurry to comply with the instructions. After his feet became grounded, he started to turn around but Bolan froze him with a 'Huh-uh! Stay! Arm's length from the car and lean on it, feet apart! And move away from that door!'

He followed instructions to the letter. A moment later another man came scrambling out feet first and went through the same routine.

Bolan moved forward and frisked them, then stepped back and ordered, 'All right, turn around and show me those faces.'

They were young faces – early twenties, Bolan guessed – and very, very frightened. The boy who had been driving reacted suddenly to something behind Bolan and yelled, 'Rachel, for God's sake tell this guy who we are!'

The girl was moving up behind Bolan. He gave her a quick snap of the eyes and growled, 'I told you to stay put.'

'I couldn't,' she replied. The voice was coming out jerky and weird – the eyes were big and sort of haunted, and she was giving Bolan that I've-never-truly-seen-you-before look.

He softened his tone and asked her, 'Do you know these people?'

'I don't recall the names,' she murmured lethargically. 'They're friends of Evie.'

83

The Beretta stayed right where it was and Bolan addressed himself to the men.

'Why were you tailing me?'

'We didn't even know it was you,' replied the driver, a blond youth. 'It was Rachel we were tailing.'

'Why?'

'Well ... if you're who I *think* you are ...' The boy glanced at his companion, then at Rachel, the gaze finally returning to rest on the tall man in buckskins with the ready gun 'We, uh, wanted to make contact with *you*.'

'Why?'

The boy shrugged and again looked at his companion.

The other youth, a dark Italian-type, told Bolan, 'We thought we might develop a mutual interest.'

Bolan replied, 'You have to talk straighter than that.'

'We wanted to join forces.'

'Against whom?'

The boy fidgeted, and the driver took it up again, and he was getting braver. 'You're smart enough to—'

Bolan snarled, 'I'm smart enough to stay alive! I can't say that for you two!'

The dark one hastened in with, 'Look, should we be standing out here in the street? What if the fuzz should happen along?'

'What do you suggest?' Bolan asked him.

'Let's find some place better to talk,' the boy replied.

'We think Evie might be in trouble,' the blond one quickly added.

The Beretta came down but remained in view. Bolan told them, 'If you guys turn sour, you'd better know ... I'd as soon wipe you as look at you.'

Rachel made an odd little sound and marched back to the VW. Bolan watched her disappear into the blowing snow, then he holstered the Beretta and told the two young men, 'Okay, let's go find that place. You'll have to help me get my vehicle back on to the street. How about yours? Think it'll run?'

The blond laughed nervously and said, 'I think it'll run okay. But you sure creamed that windshield. I wonder if my insurance pays off on acts of war?'

Bolan dug into his pocket, peeled four Harlem-fifties from a roll, and gave them to the blond boy.

'My insurance pays off on everything,' he told him. 'Will that cover it?'

The boy was surprised but he nodded his head and accepted the money. 'What happened to your bus?' he asked in a greatly relaxed tone.

'It's caught on a downslope,' Bolan told him. 'We can push it out.'

The dark youth was getting into the car. He ran his fingers along the top molding of the windshield, carefully examined the four ragged holes, and sighed loudly and announced to nobody in particular, 'That's as close as I ever want to come.'

The blond laughed again and said, 'I guess he could have just as easily brought them in dead center.'

Bolan said, 'That's right,' spun about and returned to the VW.

The sports car joined him there. Bolan ordered a sullen Rachel Silver into the driver's seat and gave her terse instructions regarding traction on slippery surfaces, then the three men got behind and pushed and heaved and grunted the laboring micro-bus on to flat surface. Then the blond grumbled something about the front wheels of his car being 'knocked out-of-line and vibrating like hell' – so Bolan took it slow and easy and the two-car caravan crept cautiously along the treacherous streets until they came to an all-night automat.

They parked the vehicles on the next side street and trudged back to the automat, got coffee and pie and took it to a quiet corner where the three men talked of politics and racketeers and dishonest public servants, and of a young girl

85

who talked too freely to possibly the wrong people. Rachel listened brooding and kept her silence. She very rarely looked at Bolan, and when she did it was with a tinge of ill-concealed disgust.

It was her turn, Bolan thought, and she was flinging something back into *his* face now. It hurt a little, sure, but if what she'd seen out on that street was enough to turn her off, then Bolan had to be thankful for early favors. Rachel did not have Viking guts – she was not a Valentina nor a Theresa, and she demanded her own image of purity from her men. He fervently wished her luck, though doubting she would find much. Under the right conditions that beast would emerge, and a woman like Rachel would find it difficult to remain 'in love' with the same guy for very long. A Jesus very rarely came along. And when he did, the Rachels of the world didn't stand a chance of latching on to him.

So Bolan inwardly felt sorry for the girl, and he saved a little of the pity for himself and for the loss of an impossible dream briefly held, and then he turned his full attention to the gory world of Executioner Mack Bolan.

He took the names and numbers of his two 'advisors', jotted pertinent notes into his little poop book, and he knew that he was entering into a new phase of his war against the Mafia.

After an hour or so he steered Rachel back to the microbus and drove her back to the high-rise where the nutty dream had begun and where it was ending.

'Short romance,' he told her as he pulled beneath the awning to let her out.

Her first words since the showdown on the street were, 'I'm sorry. I had romanticized what you are.'

'And what am I?' he asked quietly.

'A killer,' she replied.

He jerked his head forward in a curt nod. 'That's me,' he agreed. 'And if those had been killers behind us – what then? What should I have been, Rachel?'

She shivered and said, 'I'm sorry, I . . .'

He said, 'Goodbye, Rachel. Thanks for my life.'

She whispered, 'Goodbye, Mack Bolan,' then she was out and gone and Bolan knew that something fine had departed his life.

Correction. Something fine had *almost entered* his life. Thank God it hadn't quite made it. The Executioner had enough working against him – he did not need the additional complications of . . .

He threw the bus into gear and eased away from there.

A glance into the rear-view and it was gone already, lost in the great sticky gobs of winter's fruit, and back there – behind that swirling screen of white darkness – he saw in his mind's eye a thing of indescribable beauty crawling naked upon a table to escape the harsh world of men in a shadow world of gods.

'Come out, Rachel,' he murmured aloud. 'This is the only world you've got.'

CHAPTER TEN

TIES

Bolan left his vehicle in a private garage near Central Park and walked a block to a nondescript but clean budget hotel where he had registered earlier. He reached past the snoozing night clerk, took his key and walked up to the third floor room, where he sat on the bed for a few minutes mulling over the information given him by his new acquaintances, Greg MacArthur and Steve Perugia.

They were post-grad students at Columbia who had decided that political battles were better waged at City Hall rather than on campus, and they had a rather loose-knit thing going which they called CIG – City Interaction Group. A fair-sized troop of older students had been making the rounds of union halls, construction sites, docks and other workman's areas to 'rap with the hardhats,' and to attempt to find some common ground of understanding between the generations.

At first, apparently there had been a moderate success. Then the kids had set up 'rap halls' in various neighborhoods, with a program geared to 'political education.' This was not an ivory tower thing but a cold hard look at actual evidence of corruption, downright thievery, and flagrant abuses of political power. They were naming names and documenting facts, not merely shouting numbers and broad suspicions, and someone had obviously decided that they were becoming dangerous. They had been picketed, then threatened and muscled, and recently two of their halls had been bombed.

CIG did not regard this interference as a valid reaction by 'hardhats', although this is how the counterattack was made to appear. They had good reason to believe, in fact, that certain elements of the organized crime structure of the city were responsible for their harassment. There were lurking suspicions that they had been infiltrated by the enemy. MacArthur and Perugia were 'just sort of tossing around' the idea that perhaps The Executioner might wish to 'take some action' – especially since it appeared that his 'bene-factress,' Evie Clifford, 'might be in very grave danger.'

The nature or direct source of Evie's potential danger was never quite specified. Apparently MacArthur and Perugia had only a vague fear that she had talked in front of the wrong people – 'infiltrators' – or else they were trying to con Bolan into their fight. Either way, of course, Bolan had to assume the worst until he could definitely ascertain that the fears were groundless.

Also, the danger would not be confined to Evie. The other two girls were equally susceptible to a Mafia snatch. If the mob ever got the merest inkling that a path to the Ex-ecutioner led through those girls, then their lives would not be worth . . .

Bolan firmly rejected the idea. The time was nearly three o'clock, his legs were getting wobbly, and the shoulder was aching like hell. It had been a long and tiring day, and Bolan was not much given to idle worrying. He could, of course, go back and camp in the girls' living-room with a burp-gun under his arm – but his whole intent had been to carve him-self out of their lives with all haste. *If* Evie had not already compromised their security, then Bolan would certainly be doing so by continuing to hang around them. No, he could not . . .

On an impulse he went into the hall to a pay phone at the head of the stairs and called the apartment. Paula responded to about the twelfth ring, in a voice thick with sleep.

'Did Evie get home?' Bolan asked her.

'I don't know,' she replied fuzzily. 'I took a pill, and I . . . I guess I'm groggy. Just a sec. I'll go see.'

She was gone for about a minute, and her voice was much steadier when she told Bolan, 'No, she isn't back And I think Rachel is flipping out or something.'

'What do you mean.'

'I mean she's at the wailing wall, and I haven't seen that girl cry in the three years I've known her. What did you do to her?'

Bolan muttered, 'Dammit.'

'Well, what did you do?'

'Nothing, Paula. I didn't do a thing to Rachel.'

'Okay. I guess that's why she's wailing. Well, what do you think? About Evie, I mean. Should I call the police?'

'Is it unusual for her to stay out all night?' he asked.

'Not at all,' came the prompt reply, with emphasis on each word.

'Okay, then I'd say don't sweat it. But listen . . .'

'I'm listening.'

'I think it might be a good idea for you and Rachel to pack off to a hotel for a couple of days. And get Evie under your wing as soon as you can.'

A slight pause followed, then, 'You think we're in danger?'

'You've been in danger from the first moment you saw me. Yes, I think you should get out of there.'

'All right. I'll accept your judgment.'

'Call it an instinct,' Bolan told her.

'All right, and I accept that even faster. Now if I can just get Rachel to understand.'

'Tell her that I said dammit just do it.'

Paula laughed softly and said, 'Maybe you should come and tell her yourself.'

'Can't do that,' he muttered. 'I'm about out on my feet, Paula. I've got to put it down.'

'Do so carefully,' she said, and hung up.

Bolan stared at the telephone for a moment, dark thoughts of security and super-security edging through his mind, then he found another dime and placed a collect call to Pittsfield, the old home town where this war had been born. He identified himself as Sargent La Mancha, and the operator made him repeat it twice.

A sleepy voice from far away confirmed the connection on the second ring with a, 'Yeah, hello.'

The operator announced, 'I have a collect call for anyone from a Mr. Sargent La Mancha in New York City. Will you accept the charges?'

'Call from whom?' Leo Turrin asked groggily.

'The party says his name is Sargent La Mancha.'

Turrin replied, 'No, I won't accept any collect calls on this phone. Tell him to – wait a minute, I'll get that other number.'

Bolan grinned and waited while the undercover cop and Mafia under-boss dug for the number of a pay station a couple of blocks from his home. Then the familiar voice returned to the line and recited the number, and added, 'And tell him to use his own damn credit card, operator.'

Turrin hung up and the operator asked Bolan, 'Did you get that, sir?'

Bolan said, 'I sure did. Thanks, operator.' It was their own little arrangement. Bolan's voice never had to enter the hookup into Turrin's house number, but the contact was set up.

'Do you wish that I re-place to the other number now?'

'No, I'll wait a few minutes, thanks,' Bolan replied.

He returned to his room and stripped to the waist, re-moved the bandage, and looked at his wound. It was pulsing and it had a sort of an angry look to it. Bolan muttered, 'Oh hell,' and applied medication and a new bandage, then slipped the shoulder rig on to bare skin, pulled on a shirt, and went back to the telephone.

This time he paid for the call himself and Turrin's

crisp, wide-awake voice sounded pretty good to a tired and lonely warrior. Bolan told him, 'Sorry to get you out of bed.'

'In a blizzard yet,' Turrin replied. 'Temp in this phone booth right now is I guess about 69 below zero. You got snow there?'

Bolan chuckled and replied, 'Plenty. Plus many warmer activities.'

'Yeah, we're getting the vibrations all the way over here. You're rousting them pretty good, but listen – that's big-city you're fooling with now. Trying to bust New York is about equal to marching into Hanoi. You watch your step. Uh, what's on your mind?'

'I got to wondering about John-O.' Bolan was referring to his kid brother, the sole surviving relative and weakest point of Bolan's defenses. 'I was wondering if his security was still solid.'

'Yeah, it's solid,' Turrin assured him. 'He digs that military school. I don't know why, I don't think I could hack it. But he's eating it up.'

'Okay, I guess that's all I had on my mind.'

'At – what? – three in the morning? Naw, you got more than that on your mind, buddy-O.'

Bolan chuckled. 'Have you seen Valentina lately?'

'Few days ago, same time I checked the kid. She sends you her undying devotion. Don't worry, she's secure.'

'Like her work okay?'

'Yeah, she digs it too. Running an office is a bit different than running a classroom, you know, but she's there with the kid and . . .' Turrin laughed. 'She says if nothing else she'll wait until *he* grows up and marry *him*.'

Bolan said, 'Leo, I appreciate you—'

'Oh hell, don't say it. I just wish I'd stumbled on to them sooner. Don't worry, they're under heavy wraps.'

'Any money problems?'

'You kidding?'

Bolan laughed. 'Well, I dipped into the bank today and I—'

'Yeah I heard about that too. Forget it, it's all coming out of the same pocket. The kid's all right and Val is fine. So stop worrying.'

'I wasn't worrying,' Bolan said. 'I guess I just wanted to talk about them.'

'You want to try rigging a trip back this way?' Turrin asked. 'We could smuggle a meet, I think.'

Bolan said, 'Oh hell no. Don't even get me to thinking about that. Say, uh, how'd it go with you in London?'

'Clean,' Turrin told him. 'I came out smelling like a rose.'

Bolan laughed. 'I guess you're about the only one.'

Turrin also was chuckling. He said, 'Name of the game, Sarge. Listen, you watch your step in the big bad city. Something large is brewing over there and the five families are up tight, *damn* tight. So you watch it.'

'What's the brew?'

'Politics, baby. And you know how that goes.'

'Isn't it the wrong time of year for that?' Bolan asked, but something had already started crawling through his mind.

'It's always the right time for politics. You know that.'

'Yeah, but, for a big brew?'

'Well . . . yeah, I guess you're right. I don't believe they have an election coming up there for . . . oh hell, when do they vote in New York?'

'Same as other places, I guess,' Bolan replied. 'And my nose says wrong timing.'

'Yeah. Well listen. I'll see what I can pick up. You want to call me back or do you have a number there I—'

'I'll call you back. Uh, Leo. Thanks.'

'Go to hell you big slob.'

A click and a hum told Bolan that the conversation had ended. He grinned and went back to his room, and then he stopped grinning as his legs buckled under him and he had

93

to make a grab for the bedpost to remain upright. *Too much too fast, buddy,* he told himself. *Put it down, put it down.*

He put it down, clothes and all, and he was asleep before his head met the pillow, his hand resting upon the grip of the Beretta, and his mind resting upon the ties that held important lives connected to his own. And he dreamed bloody dreams.

CHAPTER ELEVEN

MAJESTY

At almost the same moment that Mack Bolan had entered the automat with his young friends, *Capo* Freddie Gambella was being awakened from a fitful sleep in his home a few miles away.

'Tommy Doctor's outside,' his night house-captain informed him in a harsh whisper. 'He's got some cunt with him that he says knows Mack Bolan.'

Gambella threw a quick look at his wife, asleep in the other bed a few feet away, and growled, 'Awright, I'll be right there.'

The captain was Angel Paleoletti, a favored veteran of some twelve years of night duty at the Gambella residence. He received his mob name from a supposed resemblance to a professional wrestler known as The Swedish Angel who was actually a Prince Charming in any close comparison with Paleoletti.

Maria Gambella openly shuddered at every sight of Angel, and she had absolutely forbade his presence in the marital bedroom. In one of the few ultimatums Maria had ever imposed upon their marriage, she had served notice to the *Capo* some years back that if she ever again awakened to find Angel Paleoletti standing over her bed, she would exit running and never return. So Gambella, in his own words a man who respected the sensitivities of womanhood, had discreetly moved the beds a few feet farther apart and impressed upon Angel the need for soft movements on nighttime errands into the boudoir.

Per this arrangement, Angel was awaiting his *Capo* in the small sitting room which adjoined the bedroom when Gambella strode out in robe and slippers, a suit of clothes slung casually over his shoulder. 'Okay, what is this now?' he asked the bodyguard.

'Tommy's outside with this cunt. He thinks you'd want to talk to her personal. You want me to let 'em in?'

'You know better, Angel,' Gambella said quietly. 'Tell Tommy I'll be out in a minute.'

'Dress warm, boss. We got a storm out there that could put out hell.'

Paleoletti slipped quietly away and Gambella took his time getting dressed, running through his mind the possible implications of this sudden break in the search for the elusive Mack the Bastard. He had known, of course, that they would tag the guy sooner or later. It wasn't possible for anything to happen in this town without the news filtering up to the king of the empire sooner or later. This was the empire state wasn't it? Damn right. And Freddie Gambella and his friends had covertly ruled it for a hell of a long time – where rule really counted, anyway. And one day soon, maybe it wouldn't be so covert. One day soon, maybe . . .

Gambella had lately been given to studying world history, with particular emphasis on Europe and the royal families who had dominated that continent and much of the world for so many centuries. The feudal kingdoms particularly fascinated the *Capo*, the parallels were so close to this blessed thing of theirs – the families of America – and he was beginning to understand where old man Maranzano had picked up his ideas for the early organization. The old boy had been a real educated gentleman, probably the only one except for Lucky Luciano who had any class at all. Gambella had secretly felt for many years that it was a damn shame for old man Maranzano to go out the way he did – he really had the right ideas.

Freddie Gambella had those very same ideas. This kingdom was going to get better organized, by God, or Freddie Gambella would die trying. But not like the old man. Hell no. It took more than ideas to fashion an empire. More than class, too. Maybe Freddie didn't have the benefit of a fancy education but he read a lot, and by God he had the benefit of thirty-five years experience of handling these people, from soldiers to *Capos*.

The old ways were okay as far as they went. They just didn't go far enough. Why should they be standing still for all this damn snooping and harassment by the feds? And these damn grand juries, these punk bastards with the holier-than-anybody-look on their faces and their damn hands just as sticky as anybody else's in the world. All these big corporations – why those bastards stole with a license that nobody ever dreamed of. They conned and robbed and gouged just like any guy on the streets, and that made them part of the game, didn't it?

Freddie Gambella was not holding still for that crap anymore. Hell no. If those guys wanted to muscle, then they'd better by God start looking for a license from the kingdom, that's what. Those senators, those congressmen, all those hunky little thieves in Washington and the legislatures, all those guys scrambling after the buck had better start doing their scrambling for licenses from the kingdom. Pretty damn soon, too. The *big thing* was by God about to happen. And it would be a chain reaction, not just here in New York but all over. The whole world, yeah.

Gambella went into the bathroom and brushed his teeth, then rinsed with mouthwash, grinned at his reflection in the mirror and told it, 'I gotta tell you this. Your Majesty, you got stinkin' breath.' He laughed, went to the closet for his topcoat, put it on and came back to inspect his image in the mirror, then he set the hat on carefully so not to muss the hair that was getting handsomely silver at the temples – yeah, real majesty – and he went out to talk to the cunt.

She was a pretty thing, all round eyed and scared out of

her skull, one tit hanging outside her coat and getting mass-aged by Earl Lattio, Tommy's top gunner.

Lattio gave him a honky kind of a smile and slid out of the car to let the *Capo* slide in. Gambella removed his hat and shook the snow off, then handed it to Tommy Doctor who was watching him smugly from the front seat. Then Gambella looked at the cute kid and told her, 'Put your titty back in before it catches cold.'

She just sat there quivering, the big eyes looking at him like maybe he was the big hero she'd been looking for to show up and rescue her. He let her see a friendly smile then reached over and tucked the tight little titty in for her and rearranged her coat.

He said, 'Didn't your momma ever tell you to wear a bra? They'll get all broke down and start sagging before you even so much as have a kid. What's your name, honey?'

Her lips moved ever so slightly and she whispered, 'Evie.'

'Is that what Bolan calls you?' he asked in a soft voice.

She just stared at him.

Tommy Doctor informed the *Capo* in that smooth college delivery, 'We've assured the young lady that our concern for Mack is the same as her's. But she's hung up on something. She simply will not believe that we're trying to help the guy.'

'Well you've got her all scared, that's why,' Gambella purred. 'Can't blame her, poor little thing, you guys playing with her titties and all that. What's your name, honey? Where do you live?'

A lengthy silence fell, then Tommy sighed and said, 'It's been this way for two hours, Mr. Gambella. We talk to her but she doesn't talk to us. I think she's a dummy.'

'And you a doctor with psychology?' the *Capo* said. 'I thought you knew how to handle people, Tommy.'

The doctor smiled and spread his hands. 'Psychology doesn't work too well on idiot mentalities,' he explained.

'Aw, don't call her no idiot,' Gambella said quietly. Some-how, in Tommy Doctor's presence he always felt compelled to talk just as streety as possible. He couldn't figure it — maybe he had to prove something to that snotty shit.

He hauled off suddenly and landed a flat-handed hay-maker against the side of the cute kid's face. It sounded like a shot and the blow propelled her over against him where she started crying with jerky, gasping little sounds. He roughly hauled her upright and held her face close to speak quietly into it.

'She's not no idiot, she's just a mixed up kid. Isn't that right, honey?'

The girl blubbered, 'Please ... Leave me alone ... I can't tell you anything. I don't *know* anything. I was just sound-ing off to sound big. You know.'

'That's the most she's said in two hours,' Tommy Doctor commented.

'Shut up, Tommy. Let me do the talking. Listen, honey, you're making me feel real unfriendly.'

The girl's lips quivered and she flared. 'You're not fooling me. And stop talking to me like I'm a child.'

'Oh, she ain't no child,' Gambella said in mock surprise. 'Those little bitty titties and she ain't no child. Maybe she's just a stunted slut.'

Evie's lips compressed and she closed her eyes as though to shut everything out. 'Better that than what you are,' she muttered.

'And what am I?' Gambella shouted. 'What am I, huh?'

She flinched away from the sudden ferocity of tone, but kept her eyes and mouth closed.

Gambella sighed loudly and turned his gaze toward the young man in the front seat. 'Where'd you pick up on this little dolly?' he asked quietly.

'She came running into Mike's about eleven o'clock. Mike's rooming with this kid from Columbia, you know that. Since about a month ago. Anyway, she comes running

99

in to see this roommate. The kid isn't there. So she wants Mike to tell her if this kid has been spilling anything about her knowing Bolan. So Mike got in touch with me. All he knows about her is that he's seen her around with those CIG punks and that her name is Evie. And she has given us nothing, but nothing.'

Gambella sighed again, then rolled down his window and called out, 'Angel! Come around to the other side and get in.'

A huge bulk crowded into the rear seat from the far side of the car, muttering profanities and brushing at clusters of snow on his clothing. The girl's eyes flashed open; she took one horrified look at the new arrival and recoiled toward Gambella.

The *Capo* chuckled and commanded his bodyguard, 'Take the little girl on your lap, Angel.'

Angel did so, hauling her on to him with two huge hands which totally spanned her waist. She resisted briefly, gurgling some horrified plea, then she gave up and sat stiffly sobbing, the blonde head wedged against the ceiling of the car.

Gambella said, 'She's going to break her neck, Angel. Cuddle the poor little thing.'

The giant bodyguard did so, dragging her head down by the hair to nestle at his throat.

Gambella squeezed her thigh and said to Tommy Doctor, 'Tell your wheelman we want to go to the weenie house. And don't hurry. Tell the other boys to stay close behind, we don't want to get separated in this weather.'

A moment later the three-car caravan was out of the drive and heading slowly toward a meat-packing plant near the waterfront. Gambella was obviously pleased with the frozen terror of his 'pigeon'. He asked Angel Paleoletti, 'Enjoying yourself, Angel?'

'Sure, boss,' the huge bodyguard replied, showing his *Capo* a hideous smile.

'Well I don't think the dolly is enjoying herself very much. You should make her feel comfortable, Angel. I think she likes to have her titties felt up. Other places too, I bet.'

Paeoletti guffawed and became busy. The girl went rigid, her eyes became sheer ice and held an unblinking focus on the domelight. The big man began squirming and a moment later announced, 'Hell, boss, this is getting me hot.'

'You'll just have to be patient, Angel,' the *Capo* told him. 'But I promise you this. You get first jump. The other boys will have to line up for sloppy seconds.'

The girl began screaming then, and they let her scream. Her frail lungs were no match for the wind-and-snow wall of silence surrounding that vehicle, and the ride to the water-front was a slow, deliberate advance into a night of terror which could not have been remotely conceived by un-sophisticated young girls such as Evie Clifford.

All three vehicles drove into the refrigerated plant at shortly before 2.00 a.m., and the hysterical girl was dragged kicking and screaming into a large room where sausages were made, begging them to listen to her and assuring one and all that she would tell them anything and everything they wished to know.

But the Kingdom of Evil observed a ritualistic attitude toward enemies of the empire, toward those who befriended such enemies, and especially toward those who could con-ceivably become future enemies of the empire. In the dogmas of this kingdom, Evie Clifford was all of these.

An image needed to be maintained, a reign of terror needed to be reinforced, an example needed to be made. So they would not listen to their pigeon – fast becoming a turkey – until she had been spreadeagled naked upon a wooden meat table in a refrigerated room, and then they listened, and a pleased *Capo* made his departure at approxi-mately twenty minutes past two o'clock, when Evie Clifford's living nightmare began in earnest. The animal shrieks of a human being in unimaginable torment persisted through the frozen time of the night and into the unseen dawn, but not one of those sounds penetrated into the ordinary world beyond those walls of the kingdom.

Long before the nightmare had ended for Evie Clifford, His Royal Majesty, Freddie the First, was telling his lady, 'Naw, go on back to sleep, everything's all right. I just went out to see the storm.'

Indeed, everything *was* all right with King Freddie. It had been a profitable night, and it would be an even more profitable morrow. It could wait 'til then, everything was falling into place beautifully, and Mack the Bastard would be screaming *his* lousy turkey-head off before the new day was ended.

The king's lady murmured sleepily and told him, 'At first I though you were that awful Angel, stealing in here like a ghost.' She turned her back and nuzzled into her pillow and added, 'The very thought fills me with horror.'

Gambella smiled and returned to his bed. Maria, he was thinking, was a bigger dope than any of them. She did not have the merest idea of what real terror was. But a lot of dopes were going to find out what it was. Damn soon, too. Just wait until things got going good into the *big thing*. Today, New York. Tomorrow, the world. The *Capo* smiled again, closed his eyes, and went peacefully to sleep.

Across town, a mindless lump of whimpering flesh was periodically screeching out everything it knew, and everything it could never possibly know, and the ears that heard did not even care anymore what was known or not known. *Man*, it is said, is the only beast that laughs at the misery of others of its own kind. There was laughter amidst those shrieks, and vile jokes, and insane inspirations for new ways to produce new shrieks. And the night of terror that surpasses all nightmares wore on and on. For Evie Clifford, the kingdom had come.

CHAPTER TWELVE

FURY

BOLAN came out of his dreams with his teeth on edge and a queasy ball in the pit of his stomach. The snow had stopped falling and it was getting daylight. A thick blanket of white lay over everything he could see from his window. He staggered down the hall, cleaned himself up, then he returned to his room and dressed for combat. He put on the thermal suit and got into a set of fatigues, then strapped on his hardware, slipped on an OD field jacket and went downstairs. The night clerk was still on duty – manning a broom in the tiny lobby. The guy did not even look up as Bolan dropped his key on the desk and strode past to the side door into the adjacent coffee shop.

He drank a pint of orange juice standing up, then he carried out coffee and Danish in a sack. The crisp air outside and the juice inside were making him feel more human by the time he reached the garage. He spent a few minutes arranging things inside the micro-bus, then he pulled on to the snow-clogged street and wondered where the hell he was going.

Something had driven him out here, something he did not even understand. Like that night near Thang-Duc when just Bolan and two Montagnard tribesmen were in night camp without shouting distance of the Ho Chi Minh Trail, when some indefinable restlessness had urged Bolan out of his hole and he'd gone off scouting the darkness alone where he'd found the Red general holding an impromptu staff meeting under the trees. The joint had turned out to be a major command post for the Northmen, and Bolan had directed air strikes that wiped the place out. All from a restless feeling like this one.

He gave the VW its head and let it go where it could along the streets of Manhattan. It was still too early for traffic – considering the street conditions, there would probably not be too many motorists even trying it. He sipped at the coffee, munched the rolls and sought out paths where the snow removal equipment had been busy. Presently he discovered that he was heading across the Harlem River and into the Bronx.

Bolan shrugged and thought, *Okay, why not?* – so, he set a course for the home of Sam the Bomber Chianti.

He took the back way in and left the VW in the alley behind the house. The sky was overcast and gray, and only the white glaze from the ground was saving the day from seeming totally dismal. A trail through the fresh snow had been walked off between the house and the garage. Sounds of activity within the latter drew Bolan to the side door; he approached with the Beretta drawn and ready.

Sam the Bomber was fussing with an assortment of suitcases, trying to fit them into the trunk of a Cadillac. He looked up and saw the Executioner standing in the doorway. Chianti's eyes blinked a couple of times and he said, 'Oh, I guess I'm surprised to see you. I guess I thought you'd be dead by now.'

'I'm not,' Bolan pointed out.

'Yeah, I see that.' Chianti went on with his packing and casually told Bolan, 'You may as well put away that gun unless you came back to finish what you started last night. I'm not armed. And I sent all my boys home. I took your advice, Bolan, I'm retiring.'

'That takes a lot of guts, Sam,' Bolan commented.

'Yeah. I heard of this guy in Washington. They say he'll put your whole family away somewheres and gives you twenty-four hour protection, for the rest of your life if he has to. A fed guy, I mean.'

'Sounds like you're getting religion.'

'No, I'm just getting smart. Look, Bolan, there's only one way to retire from this outfit, and that's with pallbearers. But I've had it up to my throat and I'm at least going to try.' He dropped a suitcase to the cement floor and turned to stare levelly at his visitor. 'I'm not even scared of you no more, Bolan. If you gotta shoot me, then go ahead. I just don't give a shit no more.'

A flicker of a smile crossed his lips and Bolan holstered the Beretta. 'I didn't come for that, Sam.'

'What did did you come for?'

Bolan shrugged his shoulders. 'I guess I just came to talk.'

'Well pardon me for saying so but I'm feeling kind of jumpy right now and I need to get going. We planned on cutting out at least an hour ago. Gotta go clear to Connecticut first, then swing back south, and the radio says the roads are a mess.'

Bolan told him, 'Don't let me delay you, Sam. Go on with what you're doing.'

Chianti turned away and again attacked the problem of the baggage. Bolan stepped over and lent a hand. The *Mafioso* glanced at him with some surprise and said, 'Thanks.'

A moment later he added, 'You know, what you were saying about religion. Don't get me wrong, I ain't been to Mass more'n twice in my whole life. But Theresa tells me it's not how you start that counts, it's how you end up. Look, Bolan. I ain't the same guy that went out on these streets thirty years ago. I mean, literally. I just ain't the same guy. A guy grows, you know. Listen, I ain't personally wiped nobody since the first time I laid my eyes on Theresa. God's truth. I don't think I could. A guy thinks he's losing his nerve, and I think what he's really doing is growing up. Know what I mean? A punk kid don't think much about stuff like that, but then one day if he's lucky he gets to be a man, and then he starts thinking about thinks like that . . . listen, just knowing Theresa made a man outta me. I owe it to her, she made me a man.'

Bolan muttered, 'I can believe that.'

'Yeah . . . well, of course, I went on with the outfit. I had to go on. But I never did no personal wipes after that. I sat on my ass and sent boys out. Somehow that's different, you know. A name on a contract, that don't mean a hell of a lot. You can kid yourself, you can say my hands are clean because hell there's no way out and I'm just doing my job so I can stay alive. And you build up all these fancy ideas to keep you going, and pretty soon you're thinking you're in a legit business. You take pride in being the best one around, and you don't let yourself think about all the hell you're doing. But listen, Bolan. Pretty soon something will always happen to make you stop and look at yourself.'

Bolan said, 'Yeah.'

'Yeah is right. I been looking at myself since you came to town. Then you came here last night, and just like a dead man I saw it all rolling past my eyes, I mean my whole life, and God I felt like crying inside. And it was too late. That was the hell of it, see. Too late. Then you tell me, go on Sam, go get some coffee and think about it. Jesus I'd already thought about it, my whole damn life in a flash past my eyes – Theresa and the kids, and what a rotten bastard I really been to have people like that caring if I lived or died . . . I guess you know what I mean.'

'I know what you mean,' Bolan assured him.

They finished stowing the luggage. Chianti was standing there looking at him with wondering eyes, and finally Bolan asked him, 'Where do I find Freddie Gambella, Sam?'

The guy sighed, looked at his hands, and said, 'Thirty years we been buddies. I mean, yeah, he's always been the boss, there's been no mistake ever about that . . . but we been buddies. He's the godfather of my kids. He sat up with me all night in the hospital when the first one was coming. Theresa was having a hard time, so Freddie sat there and held my hand all night long to keep me in my skull.'

Bolan told him, 'I'm sorry, Sam. But I have to know.'

'Well wait. Lemme tell you. We've went on vacations together, the four of us, and sometimes Maria insisted we take the kids along because she couldn't have none herself, and she said our kids were her kids. I mean, this is the kind of friends we've been, Bolan. Or I thought so. But listen, I think Freddie's going insane. I mean that. Or else he always has been.

'Listen, Bolan, last night you had a feeling for Theresa, a perfect stranger, but you had a feeling for her. Wouldn't you think the godfather of our kids would have some feeling like that? No, there ain't no feeling like that, Bolan. Freddie would throw me to the wolves, and he'd throw Theresa too, and I bet his own godkids. You wanta know where to find Freddie? Well, I'm going to tell you where, Bolan. And not because I'm afraid of you neither. You know what I been thinking? I been thinking that Freddie has been on to me for a long time. I mean, me not wanting blood on my hands. I think he's trying to *keep* blood on my hands, Bolan. Don't ask me why, I just think that. I think he don't want to ever let me off the hook, he's gonna keep me bloody right to my grave if he can.'

Bolan nodded understandingly and offered Chianti his notebook. 'He's got four addresses, Sam, I only want one.'

'That's the one I'm going to give you.' Chianti took the book and pencil from Bolan and laboriously printed an address in large crude block letters. He sighed heavily and returned it to Bolan, then told him, 'Look there's something else you need to know, I mean I guess I owe it to you to tell you. Freddie found hisself a turkey last night.'

A nerve ticked in Bolan's cheek and a chill raced down his spine. Woodenly he muttered, 'Who was the turkey, Sam?'

Chianti shook his head. 'I really don't know and I didn't

ask, because I didn't want to know. But one of the boys called me a couple of hours ago, and he said they had a turkey down at the weenie house, and wouldn't I like to come down? I told him hell no and I hung up. But that's why I was kinda surprised to see you walk up. I figured they'd got to you by now.'

'Where is this weenie house?' Bolan asked tightly. Something was shrieking up and down his nervous system and he knew now why that Thang-Duc restlessness had driven him out into the gray dawn to seek something nameless and unimagined.

'If you're thinking of going, it's too late,' Chianti was telling him. 'This was a couple of hours ago, and it was turkey already.'

'Where's the weenie house?' Bolan growled ominously.

Chianti sighed and took the notebook back, printed another oversize address, and returned it to the tall man who was suddenly wearing the death mask again. Those eyes had cemetery markers blazing out from the cold depths . . . Sam shivered inwardly and wondered if he'd said the wrong thing.

'Listen, wait a minute, Bolan. If you go to hit Freddie, use the side entrance on 155th Street. Pull up to the gate and stop with your front wheels on the little metal cleats, then give three quick flashes of your headlights. The gates will open automatically and that driveway will take you right into the carport. And Jesus – lookout. Freddie has a big palace guard.'

Bolan jerked his head and said. 'Thanks, Sam. Good luck getting to Washington.'

Then he was out of there and running for the VW. His blood was ice, his head was a spinning web of anguish and self-recrimination, and he was praying over and over to a nameless God that it would all turn out to be a nightmare, or that he was dead and in hell. There just could not be another turkey on Mack Bolan's soul.

He parked the micro-bus at the big sliding door marked RECEIVING – and stepped to the rear for weapons. The chattergun, an efficient little folding-stock burper handling .25 calibre exploders, went around his neck and he stuffed extra clips into the pockets of the fatigues. Next he strapped on the web belt with the grenades still clipped to it, then added an army .45 in a flap-holster.

The door slid back easily and he walked in with the chattergun ready. Two cars were parked inside, one of them a big limousine with jumpseats, but there was nobody around. The working day had not yet begun – apparently the work of the night had not ended, either.

He followed his instincts and went through a long hall-like room with refrigerated beef-quarters dangling from automated meat-hooks, and came into a large room with cutting tables and a variety of machinery. Two guys were dragging a weighted bag across the floor toward a doorway at the far end, guffawing over something very funny.

They looked up together, saw Bolan and froze, and he zipped them with a blazing criss-cross from the chattergun that flung them spinning through the open doorway. He followed through with a running charge that sent him hurtling over their sprawling bodies at about the same moment that six other guys in the next room were coming unglued and reacting to the gunfire.

Someone shouted, *'Bolan!'* – and people were flinging themselves every which way clawing at gunleather. He caught a big ape of a guy with a face like Godzilla in a climbing burst from the guts up, that laid the guy wide and split the ugly face open at the eyes, then everything the ape had inside seemed to be exploding out of him.

Another two were scrambling away from a cutting table and running for a walk-in freezer. Bolan let them go for the moment and swung on to another pair who were diving for the cover of a metal cabinet. He helped them get there with a sustained burst from the chattergun that sent them tumbling and mutilated in a grotesquely flopping sprawl. One of them was still alive enough to be mouthing screams, but Bolan's attention was being demanded by the sixth man, a youngish guy with a long-barreled hogleg throwing fire everywhere except at Bolan.

The burper put out a floor-level string that cut the guy's ankles away from him, then climbed in a figure-eight that kept him from going down right there and flung him in a heap a couple of bodylengths back.

Then Bolan released the chopper and let it dangle by the shoulder cord, circled quickly to the walk-in box and pulled on the heavy door. It cracked open and a hail of slugs in rapidfire from two pistols thwacked harmlessly into the thick wood. Bolan pulled the pin on a grenade, held it for a moment, tossed it in through the crack in the doorway, then stepped quickly aside.

A panicky voice within screeched, *'Lookout, it's—'*

Then the wall rumbled and the floor moved slightly beneath Bolan's feet. The massive door swung open with a rush and a body was ejected in a flight that deposited it in a smoking heap several yards into the room. Bolan took a look inside and saw that the other guy had been blown in the opposite direction and impaled on a meat hook.

The dying screams down by the metal cabinet were becoming more frantic, but again Bolan's attention was diverted from that agony by a blood-freezing sight on a nearby cutting table. He had passed that table a moment earlier, but with his attention directed into the firefight he'd thought the hunk of meat lying there was a beef quarter or something. But beef quarters did not grow long golden hair, and Bolan knew now that it was not beef. It was turkey, and something was shrinking Bolan's guts and clawing at him from the inside.

He stepped jerkily to the table and gazed down upon what was left of Evie Clifford. The dead eyes stared back at him. They had to. The eyelids had been sliced away. And even through the coagulated blood that was brimming those horrified sockets Bolan could see the agony and the accusation and the mirror of his own guilt and neglect.

They had battered out her front teeth and committed awful atrocities upon the once lovely torso, and what they had done below that point sent Bolan's usually steady mind into a spin through insanity.

His chin dropped to his chest, his eyes closed on the terrible scene, and he groaned, 'Oh . . . *God*!'

Then he went down to the screeching man and shoved the hot muzzle of the chattergun into the wide open mouth and he pulled the trigger and let the gun burp until the clip was empty, and somewhere in there the screaming stopped. He dropped a marksman's medal into the gaping well of blood, and reloaded, and went deliberately from body to body and repeated the routine.

Somewhere along that bloody trail his mind began to clear, and when he had completed the senseless and futile acts of revenge upon the dead, he found a bolt of cheesecloth, and he carefully wrapped Evie Clifford's pitiful remains, and tenderly carried her out of hell and gently placed her in the rear of the micro-bus.

His cheeks were twitching and the eyes were brimming with a salty discharge of emotion as he climbed in behind the wheel and sat there a moment willing his mind to find its place. A city bus pulled up at the corner of the building and began disgorging workers in white uniforms. Bolan watched them go into the packing plant, and he found himself wondering idly what they would think about their latest consignment of meat.

Then he swiped away the moisture of his eyes with brutal knuckles, put the VW into gear and headed back into the jungle of his rage.

He knew that a part of him had died with Evie Clifford. There was not much left, at the moment, but icy hatred and a blazing fury.

They should not have done this to Evie.
He was going to tell them so.
He was going to tell it to Freddie Gambella.

MONSTROSITIES

BOLAN eased the VW along the avenue in a slow recon of
the big place on the corner. It was one of those turn of the
century monstrosities where the architect had obviously
been unable to decide if he felt Victorian, or Gothic, or just
frivolous. The result was a three-story jumble of bay
windows and cathedral-stained glass, square columns and
turreted corners, wood and stone, and a roofline featuring
everything from gables to minarets, with an occasional gar-
goyle thrown in just to make sure there was something for
everyone. It was an anachronism from a flamboyant age, and
Bolan could understand how a guy who had muscled his way
up from a two-room coldwater flat in East Harlem would be
impressed with such a joint. Even in old age it reeked of
wasteful opulence and flagrant power – yeah, that joint was
Freddie Gambella from the stained-glass cathedral windows
to the gargoyles leering down from the gabled eaves. The
whole production was set off from the street by a rock wall
with ancient iron spikes. The pedestrian gate alone had
more steel in it than his VW.

Bolan passed on around the corner on to 155th and went
through the routine suggested by Sam the Bomber. Sure as
hell the massive gates swung open and Mack Bolan swung in
with his daisied micro-bus. He'd seen two guys walking the
snowdrifts of the yard in bulky overcoats, and he rolled
down his window to wave at the nearest one as he tooled
along the drive. Another guy ran up as he pulled into the

carport, gave Bolan a hard look, and said, 'What the hell're you do—'

He'd had time by then to get a good look at that cold face and had decided to stop talking and start slapping leather, but Bolan's hardware was already nosing up over the door panel. The Beretta spat out a sizzler that splatted in directly between the eyebrows and the guy went down like he'd been poleaxed.

Bolan had the door open and was swinging down to the ground when the yardman came slugging up through the snow. He was looking at the fallen man, not at Bolan, and he cried, 'What'd you do, idiot, run him down?'

The Executioner replied, 'Yeah,' and ran another one down with a bullet behind the ear, and the guy fell over atop the first one.

The second yardman was coming around the corner of the house, and his first view of Bolan was looking up along the fully-extended black blaster. He recoiled from the unsettling view, but not fast enough, then a pair of Parabellums found their mark and punched the guy over into drifted white snow that quickly turned red.

Five seconds later, Fury was standing at the door to the little concrete-block house which was joined to the main house by the carport. Bolan kicked the door open and stepped in with the chattergun at full throttle. Two very surprised diners seated at a table in their underwear were the first in the receiving line so they received a .25 caliber explosive wreath about their throats and chests.

Another reared up off a cot and was immediately laid backdown with a mouthful of metallic pacifiers.

A large fat one with a protruding belly stumbled to an open bathroom door, stark naked and gawking at Death through puffs of shaving lather. The burst split him from groin to throat, the protruding belly opened and seemed to deflate, the fat one fell back into the toilet bowl and wedged there.

Agony stepped out and glided to the rear door of the mansion. A big man in full dress wearing an apron had moved to the door in curiosity over the rattling sounds from the blockhouse. He fell away in a swift back-pedal as Bolan came through, the guy threw two slices of toast at Doom and pivoted about to make a run for the other door. The Beretta coughed twice and the big man missed the turn into the doorway and crashed over a table, sliding to the tiled floor in a mess of orange juice and scrambled eggs from a breakfast tray.

Remorse went on, through the pantry and the deserted dining-room into a darkened hallway. An inside man who had obviously been seated near the door at the far end had abandoned his station to investigate the noise from the kitchen. He approached to within ten feet of Disaster before he recognized the tall figure with the taut face and gleaming teeth, then he just froze and stared, perched across his stride like one of those stop-action shots on NFL Today.

'Bolan?' he asked unbelievingly.

Belief went up to him, pressed the heated silencer of the Beretta against his throat, pulled a snubbed .32 out of a shoulder holster, dropped it to the floor, and an icy voice told the guy, 'You guessed it. Now let's play twenty questions. How many hardmen in the house?'

'F-four,' the guy wheezed.

'Let's just play *one* question,' Bolan suggested in that graveyard voice, the Beretta sinking deeper into the shrinking throat.

The hardman expelled whistling air through the constricted larynx and whispered, 'Andy – Andy in th' kitchen. Fixin' breakfast for Mrs. Gambella, Me, Two upstairs. Hall, each end.'

'Nobody on the third floor?'

'No. Not used. Nobody on the third floor.'

Reluctant Mercy growled, 'Thanks,' and jerked a knee into the quaking man's gut, then slammed the butt of the

115

Beretta against the back of his head as he sank toward the floor. Bolan stepped around the unconscious form and proceeded on through into a huge reception hall at the front. Folding doors of heavy paneling were at each side, easily twenty feet tall. A mahogany staircase curved up around the rear and broadened to a landing about forty feet above.

Grim Determination went up, the Beretta holstered and a fresh clip clicking into the chattergun. This would not be so simple if the upstairs men were alert. One to each side could be bad news.

He ascended swiftly, moving on light feet with the burper at half mast, and he hit the second-floor hall at full gallop. A dim figure coming to stiff attention in the distance to his left drew first fire as Bolan crouched and swung into the attack. He laced that end of the hallway with a spiral burst right on target — and kept on going around, twisting to the floor in a corkscrew then laying into the other flank from semiprone.

A heavy man was dancing around down there, trying to become disengaged from an easy chair that was splintering into pieces around him and with him. A revolver roared through the lighter chatter of Bolan's weapon and a slug thwacked into a post beside his head, but it was the one and only response to his blitz. The guy was coming apart — spouting blood in streams and still trying to get off another shot. Bolan massaged his trigger lightly once again, the guy fell over backwards, crashed through the chair, and the battle was over.

A shrill female voice was yelling something from behind a door just opposite Bolan's position. He turned the knob, kicked the door open and advanced into an elegant room with Persian carpeting and swank furnishings. It was part of a bedroom suite — a sitting room, Bolan supposed they'd call it. Off to one side was a dressing-room and beyond that a gleaming bath. Dead ahead through a fancily carved doorway lay the master's chamber, and this was where Vengeance had been headed all the while.

116

The woman yelled something else in an hysterical falsetto as Bolan entered, then she clamped it off in mid-squawk to stare at the intruder with a terror that seemed to keep growing. She was sitting up in the bed with a newspaper – a cup and a silver coffeepot on a tray in front of her. The other bed was rumpled and tossed but empty.

Seething Hatred peered under both beds, into the closets and even out the windows and on to the eaves outside, while the woman was sitting there in a frozen curl and staring at him with open mouth.

He turned to her with a deep growl and asked, 'Where's Freddie?'

The woman was about fifty, and she knew Bolan all right, but she was not made of Theresa's stuff. She began screaming in breathless yelps – he had to go over and slap her a couple of times to shut her up.

'Where's your husband?' he again demanded.

'I don't know!' she yelled back. 'Isn't he here?'

Frustration swept the bed-tray away and it hit the floor with a crash and a splattering of coffee, then he pulled the covers away from her and dragged her out of the bed. She wore a heavy nightgown and a short bedjacket and she was a pretty goodsized gal, thick through the chest like an opera singer with hips to match. She'd been a beauty once, though, and traces of it still lingered there behind the misshapen flesh.

He pulled her terrified face close to his and snarled into it. 'All I want is Freddie. Now you tell me damn quick where to find him.'

No, she was no Theresa or Valentina. There was guilt in that face, knowledge of evil and a complicit acceptance of it, and Bolan had seen her kind before also. Somehow he just could not see Maria and Theresa as buddies, and he wondered just how much of that idea had been Sam Chianti's own.

'H-he left about a h-half hour ago,' she was chattering. 'I don't know where, Holy Mother I don't know.'

Yeah, Holy Mother, take care of her murderous jackal of a psychotic husband so he could continue to rape the world for Maria's fancy houses and animal comforts. Bolan had to wonder, could she really know what went into the upkeep of an empire like Gambella's?

The woman must have read Bolan's thoughts. 'Now listen, mister,' she told him in a voice that was struggling hard for control. 'You have it all wrong about Fred. Why don't you just leave him alone? You're the one causing all the trouble. Fred is a good man, and he only does what he has to do to protect his business. Any man would do that. Any man will fight to protect his investments.'

Maybe she *didn't* know. Maybe she'd insulated herself from the reality in much the same manner as Chianti had described his own adjustments. Growling Outrage told her, 'Okay, lady, you asked for it. I'm going to show you one of this good man's latest investments.'

He dragged her out of there and down the curving mahogany, and she was protesting and pleading all the way in a choked garbling of words. Bolan just couldn't feel sorry for her, all the sorrow had been wrung out of him in a confrontation with one of her husband's turkeys.

She gasped and hyperventilated as Bolan pushed her past the fallen man in the downstairs hall, and she nearly came all the way unglued when she had to step over the bloodied Andy-eggs-juice cocktail on the kitchen floor.

Bolan steered her out the door and she cried, 'I can't go out like this!'

He ignored her protest, pulled her over to the VW, opened the side doors, and made her crawl inside. Then he dragged her back to where the mutilated girl lay, and gently he unwrapped the shroud of cheesecloth, and as Maria Gambella became confronted with a reality without insulation she came apart then and there. She fought Bolan for the doorway, shrieking and scratching and clawing her way

118

out of there, and she went out in a tumble, squawking as she hit the ground.

Bolan jumped out behind her, pulled her to her feet, then helped her inside the house. He put her in a chair in the dining room and brought her some water. She ignored the offer, staring at the floor with a frozen face and panting raggedly with her exertions.

Quietly, Bolan told her, 'That's the kind of business your husband promotes, Mrs. Gambella. And I want to talk to him about it. Now you tell me where he is.'

'You go straight to hell,' she panted.

'You tell me, or I'm going to carry that pathetic side of meat into this house, and I'm going to put her in your bed, and I'm going to tie you in there with her.'

The woman's eyes rolled toward her forehead and the blood drained from her face. In a choked voice, she said, 'All right, smart guy. I hope you do find him, and that will be the end of you. But I don't know where he went, and you can believe that or not. He just said he had a date with some girls, and I wouldn't be a bit surprised if he did. He's a *man,* my husband. *A real man*!'

Utter Disgust told her, 'He sure is, Mrs. Gambella.'

But there was more than disgust in that tortured mind, there was a sudden shivering fear that Maria Gambella had told him quite a bit more about her husband's plan of the day than she'd realized.

He told her, 'You better call the fire department.'

'Why should I call the . . .?'

'Because I'm going to burn down your lousy palace, Mrs. Gambella.'

Bolan went back through the kitchen, and the woman came scurrying after him.

'What are you talking about?' she yelled.

He went on to the VW and she hopped anxiously about just outside the house, loudly wanting to know what he'd meant by that remark as he reached into the bus and hauled out the bag of incendiaries.

He delayed long enough to kneel beside one of the fallen yardmen and strip off his overcoat. He threw it at Gambella's Queen and ordered her to put it on, then he picked up his bag and went back inside the house. He scattered the incendiaries in appropriate places, and when he returned to the carport the woman was gone. He climbed into the VW, backed around, and got out of there.

A cluster of curious people were on the sidewalk staring toward the house, attracted probably by the earlier rattling of gunfire. It had been a quick hit, all considered, but he had overplayed his timetable by several minutes and as Bolan knew the cops would be along any time now he wasted no further time in clearing the area.

As he made the turn off of 155th Street, he glanced back over his shoulder and saw flames leaping into the sky and he smiled grimly over small compensations and turned his mind toward the larger ones.

First, though, he had to stop by an East Side highrise to try his hand at reading some Manhattan Indian signs. He shivered, wondering again about the identity of the girls Freddie Gambella had gone off so early in the morning to 'date'.

You'd better not, Freddie, he was thinking. He would follow that guy all the way to hell, and if he found him there he would gladly stay to personally supervise the eternal torment of that monster.

Yeah, Freddie Gambella was a monstrosity, just like that burning joint of his back there. So was his old lady, and so was anybody and everybody who made a living from the Gambella 'business enterprises'.

'You'd just better not, Freddie,' Bolan murmured aloud. The Executioner was some kind of a monstrosity himself.

CHAPTER FOURTEEN

OPTIONS

IT was getting on to mid-morning. The streets were in fair condition and the big city was humming into the day as though the storm had never come. Bolan had been driving aimlessly allowing his mind to settle back into sanity. He had a dead girl on his hands, and he had several large-size problems to be considered on behalf of the living. He knew that he had to *concentrate* on the living, and just now that meant Paula and Rachel.

Bolan's only hope was that the two girls had made it out of that apartment and to a safe place before Gambella learned of their existence. It was a frail hope. There was no doubt whatever Evie had told everything Gambella had wanted her to tell, and she had probably told it very early into the night of her torment.

It had taken the kid a long time to die, that much had been quite obvious. Bolan never ceased to marvel at how long a healthy body could sustain brutal assaults upon non-vital functions and go on living. Death had unquestionably come to Evie Clifford as a slow advance into massive shock, brought on by continued torment and a gradual loss of blood. The monsters had known their business, and they'd kept her alive and aware for one hell of a long time.

Bolan's soul shuddered with the memory of it and he asked himself for the thousandth time why it had to happen to a sweet and harmless kid like Evie. Then he shook Evie Clifford out of his mind and returned again to the problems of the living.

In her place, he began establishing a rationale for Gambella. The guy either had the girls or he didn't. Either he got
to them, or he *could not* get to them, or he *decided against*
snatching them. How would a smart *Capo* handle the information he'd rung out of Evie?'

Bolan damned himself for not having the foresight to establish a contact schedule with Paula during that final
conversation. Bolan did not have the personnel resources to
check out every hotel in Manhattan, not even the most
obvious ones. Gambella did have. If he missed the girls at
their apartment, he could damn soon cover every hotel in the
city.

But did Gambella really want the girls? Did he actually
need them? Bolan knew what *he* would do in Gambella's
place. He would not touch those girls, not right away. First
he'd put them under close surveillance, he'd bug their apartment, their salon and their telephones, he'd stake-out their
home and their place of work, he'd get a feel into everyone
who knew them and the places they went – then he'd just sit
back and wait for Bolan to show.

And if the pigeon did not come along in a reasonable time,
then he would go ahead and snatch the girls, and he'd find a
way to let Bolan know that he had them, and he'd challenge
the guy to come and get them before he made turkeys out of
them.

Yes, that would be the strategy. The enemy knew Bolan as
well as Bolan knew them. He had to figure that. They knew
that he would not run away and leave his friends at the
mercy of the turkeymakers.

Okay, so how about a rationale for the quarry? How
would a smart Executioner counter such a strategy? That
problem was complicated, of course, by the knowledge that
this was no mere game of chess. The lives of two good
women could be dangling in the balance and . . .

Bolan snapped off that line of thought and tried to align
himself away from the emotional aspects. This was a

battlefield problem in strategy and tactics, moves and countermoves – nothing else. He had to keep it that way, unless he wished to defeat himself.

Okay, so here's what a smart pigeon would do. First, he would assume that Gambella *could have* snatched the girls – and then he would remove to every extent possible whatever options the other side might have. He would. ... Yes, by God, he would.

Bolan smiled grimly at the idea that was forming in his mind. Yes. It would be the most logical countermove.

He drove directly to Receiving Hospital and left the shrouded figure of Evie Clifford on an ambulance dock, in full view where he knew she would quickly be discovered, and he left a note folded into a mutilated little hand. The note identified her and explained what had happened to her – by whom, where, and why. It also contained a solemn promise that justice was going to be done – by whom, and against whom.

He pulled away to a discreet holding position to watch the scene through binoculars until the body was discovered. He saw the orderly or whatever recoil from the grisly find, and he watched the uniformed cop who came charging out of the emergency entrance, and he saw the cop pulling the note out of the dead fingers.

He made a mental note of the time, then he went away, his hands and his mind done with the beloved dead. He cruised slowly toward the apartment building, and when he arrived there he mentally tipped his hat to the New York's Finest as he noted the police cruisers clustered about the garage entrance. He smiled as he went on by. If the Mafia had been hanging around, they weren't now. One of Gambella's options was gone. Maybe even all of them, if the cops should also lock onto Paula and Rachel to tuck them away into protective custody.

Again he noted the time, then stopped at a phone booth ten minutes away and called the Lindley apartment. A guarded male voice answered the second ring, and Bolan distinctly heard the extension phone also click into the line.

Bolan identified himself and asked to speak to the head cop. A whispered consultation followed, then another voice replied, 'This *is* the head cop. What the hell are you up to, Bolan?'

'Are the girls there?' he asked.

'Why don't you come and see for yourself?'

'No way,' Bolan replied coolly. 'That's why I sent you. I figure Freddie has the joint sealed.'

Bolan could here the cop breathing and he could *feel* the cogs moving in that mind. The heavy voice told him, 'Yeah, I see your point. Look, fella . . .'

Bolan said, 'Lindley and Silver are in deep trouble. This is no time for fine points of law. You talk to me and talk straight, or those girls could end up like the other one.'

The cop sighed heavily into the mouthpiece and said, 'Okay, Bolan. Temporary truce, with none of the finer points of law. How do you know that Gambella was behind this gruesome bit of work? Do you have evidence? Do you admit to rubbing out the eight guys down at Kluman Brothers?'

Bolan growled, 'Look, you must know I didn't call just to pass the time of day or to give you a telephone fix on me. So let's keep this simple and to the point.'

'Okay, Bolan. Do you know the whereabouts of the two young women, Lindley and Silver?'

'No. I contacted them about three this morning and suggested they find a place to hide. I think I might have been too late. What does it look like there?'

The cop sighed again. He obviously was not enjoying his role as informant to a wanted criminal, but he carried on. 'Not too good,' he muttered. 'The place is in disarray, stuff thrown around, a half-packed suitcase in the living-room. It could be a snatch. Or it could be simply a hurried departure.'

'Check the hotels,' Bolan suggested. 'And check *Paula's Fashions*, over in the—'

'Already did,' the cop snapped back. 'Car just reported back, the shop didn't open today.'

Bolan said, 'Find them, dammit,' and he hung up.

Score another point for cops, he was thinking. They knew the Mafia mentality also, and they would be moving hell to find those girls.

So Gambella could still have those options. Bolan returned to the VW and headed into the next step of the counter-strategy.

At eleven o'clock on that chill Wednesday morning in New York, the Executioner invaded the Mafia heartland. Using information contained in his 'poop book' some of it gathered from the CIG informants, MacArthur and Perugia, he 'hit' three establishments in quick succession, all controlled by the Gambella Family, in a lightning blitz which left certain elements of the New York scene with a severe case of the shakes.

The first strike was against a 'union hall' in the garment district. It was a phoney union, according to Bolan's information, existing on paper only with the profits extorted from workers and employers alike. It was owned and operated by one of Gambella's lieutenants.

Bolan double-parked outside the office building where the union was headquartered, took an elevator to the third floor, calmly walked into the office and shot dead at their desks the three officers who comprised the 'governing board', then handed a marksman's medal to the stupefied female stenographer and walked out.

Twenty minutes later he struck again, this time at the Manhattan offices of Schweiberg, Fain, and Marksforth – purportedly an investment brokerage firm but actually the funnel through which Gambella's illict wealth was spread into the legitimate business world. The firm went abruptly out of business at 11.22 A.M. that Wednesday in December, the partnership dissolved by mutual death, its records consumed by a fire of incendiary origin. Again, a tall man in army fatigues and an OD field jacket pressed a marksman's medal into the shaken palm of a female employee before he calmly departed the scene.

At a few minutes past noon, in the back room of a neighborhood restaurant on 144th Street, a weekly 'business luncheon' of the Upper Manhattan Protective League was disrupted by an obvious lack of protection. This group, consisting of neighborhood politicians and musclemen, was severely depleted of active membership by the sudden appearance of two fragmentation grenades on the menu. A tall man in army combat dress stopped at the cashier's counter and settled the property damages with a thousand dollars in cash and a marksman's medal.

At one o'clock, Bolan telephoned the news room of a New York television station. In a recorded interview given at that time, he described the atrocities commited upon the body of Evie Clifford, spoke of his fears for 'two of her friends', and revealed his plans for the Gambella Family of New York.

The interview was aired on local television at 1.30, and the cool tones of the Executioner were heard on local radio outlets repeatedly throughout that day.

'I am going to destroy the Gambella Family. One by one, crew by crew, business by business – I am going to wipe them. I will not be bought off or scared off by threats against defenseless and innocent persons, and if one more sweet kid is turned to turkey because of me, then these turkeymakers are going to discover what a real nightmare is all about. There is no escape for these people. I knew each of them, I know where they go and what they do, and I am going to hunt them down, all of them, and I am going to execute them.'

The sensational story was quickly picked up by television and radio networks, and two New York daily newspapers came out with special editions featuring pictures and details of the carnage at Kluman Brothers Packing Company, scene of Evie Clifford's grisly murder; the destruction of the Gambella mansion and the added carnage there; the three strikes of the late-morning blitz across Manhattan. Speculation also linked the six bodies found in Brooklyn on Tuesday with Mack Bolan's presence in town, and the body count of 'at least thirty-five dead *Mafiosi*' was given considerably more attention than the instance of a single innocent victim.

And the big city settled back with an air of expectancy, a frantic air in some quarters, waiting to see what would happen next.

Bolan had given the *Capo* – indeed, all the *Capos* of New York City – another option to think about.

CHAPTER FIFTEEN

TUTTI

'SURE, I'm getting feed-in from both sides of the stream,' Leo Turrin's voice reported across the connection from Pittsfield. 'You're really rattling the cage there, buddy. Hey, it's all over television here, even. You going nuts or something?'

'Maybe,' Bolan replied gloomily. 'So what'd you find out?'

'First of all, let's take the matter of official reaction. Do you know how many cops the city of New York has to throw against you, my blitzing buddy? At last count, roughly thirty-two thousand. That's a lot of men in blue, more than enough to populate an average American city.'

'They haven't bothered me yet,' Bolan muttered.

'Well, they've known you were in town since that first little fracas at Midtown Station. But they're a pretty cool bunch, those New York cops. They have so much crime there, on a minute-to-minute basis, that they just play it by the numbers and everything waits its turn, even a Mack Bolan. But your turn has come, buddy. You're on the hot list, and you can bet your ass that right now those guys are gearing up to stop you. There's an unofficial quote shoot on sight unquote order covering you at this moment. You're getting the mad-dog treatment.'

'Okay, that's one,' Bolan said. 'What's two?'

'Two is Freddie Gambella and Company. I hear the guy is frothing at the mouth – throwing tantrums all over the place. You torched his beloved palace, you rotten shit, and stamped out the guard besides, plus terrifying his lady. Very undignifying, Sarge, for a *Capo*.'

Bolan said, 'Yeah. So what's new?'

'What's new is that you'd better get the hell away from there, and via the quickest means. Try a time machine and go back to the seventeenth century or something.'

'Get serious,' Bolan growled.

'I'm as serious as I can get. I never saw such a guy. I thought I'd seen it all *here*, when you went after Sergio. Then when I saw what was left after the hit on Miami Beach I told myself, why hell no Leo, *now* you're seeing it all. So here you are taking on the City of New York, complete with its Five Families and fellow travelers. When do you figure your luck is going to run out, buddy?'

Bolan was being gently chided, he knew it – but he didn't mind. He chuckled and told his friend, 'I guess I'm like the New York cops. I have so much crime on my hands I have to take it minute by minute and luck by lucky break. You know what I want to hear, Leo. How's the mob reacting to my Tarzan act?'

'Oh they're impressed. Jittery as hell. A lot of 'em are suddenly finding reasons why they have to go out of town for awhile. And I get the feeling that a lot of displeasure is building against Gambella. High level displeasure. The other bosses, I hear, are quite concerned because of . . .'

'Because of what?'

'Aw, shit. And me a double agent.'

'Uh-huh. Okay, you started to spill. So out with it. What's going on that I should know about?'

'Dammit, Mack, there are some things—'

'You know better. I need every item of intelligence I can get.'

There was a brief pause, then Turrin's breath hissed across the line in a lengthy sigh. 'Okay. Some day I'm going to get nailed up over this double-agent stuff. Why did I have to add *you* to my list of tragedies?'

'Give, Leo.'

'May I first impose on our friendship to give you a bit of very sober advice?'

'You may,' Bolan told him. 'Go on, impose.'

'You're a dead man. You know that, don't you? I mean, not to be morbid but just to face facts, from one friend to another. You're a dead man.'

Bolan said, 'Thanks, friend . . . but . . . yeah okay, I accept that.'

'Okay. So it's just a matter of time before your death certificate becomes official. You may have another day, another week, another month – or maybe just another hour. So what the hell are you accomplishing?'

It was Bolan's turn for silence. Presently he replied, 'I don't know, Leo. I've just been playing it by ear, trying to stay alive, hoping to carry the fight against this Goddamned cancer that a lot of people in this country still think doesn't exist. They're all going to wake up one day and find it eating them alive. I don't know, Leo. What the hell do you mean, what am I accomplishing? I'm harassing the hell out of them if nothing else. What kind of question is that to ask a dead man?'

Turrin chuckled. 'Okay, it was a leading question. You've been waging a war of attrition – like in 'Nam, right? With the odds at about a million to one. So who do you think is going to win this war, Sarge?'

'I never hoped to win it, Leo,' Bolan told him. 'The damned outfit is omnipresent, omniscient, and omnipotent. I know that. It's like fighting heaven. You can spit in God's face fifty times a day every day, but you know that in the end it's all going to go his way. Okay. So I've just been pushing sand around on the beach, not trying to fill the ocean with it.'

'So why don't you start filling?'

'Yeah, okay.'

'I'm serious. You think about it. And think about this.

Have you ever heard the expression, *Cosa di tutti Cosa?*'

'No. I've heard of *Capo di tutti Capo*, the boss of all the bosses, but I hear that one's a thing of the past.'

'It is, but not the *tutti Cosa*. It's a thing of the future, or so billed, and it roughly translates as *the thing of all the things*.'

'Or Big Thing,' Bolan suggested.

'You've heard of it, then.'

'Not actually, no. A whisper somewhere, maybe that's all. Is this what you weren't going to spill?'

'That's it.'

'So? Give.'

'I already gave. It's all I know. It has something to do with politics, and I think I told you this morning that something big was brewing. Well, that's what's brewing, *Cosa di tutti Cosa*. So if you really want to accomplish something in New York, why don't you look into that?'

'I'm no detective. I'm an infantryman.'

Turrin laughed. 'Look, Sarge. It's common knowledge that the mob is everywhere, in everything. They've got congressmen, legislators, mayors, and maybe even a couple of governors. They've infiltrated all levels of the legit business world, and they've got labor unions, a good chunk of the entertainment industry, civil servants up the kazoo, entire political machines – anyplace where money is king – and hell, it's like you said, they're a cancer and they're eating into everything. So far as I know, they do not presently *own* any U.S. Senators or White House advisors or members of the cabinet. *So far as I know*, they've never had a piece of a U.S. President, or a seat on the Supreme Court. *So far as*–'

'Okay, I get the picture,' Bolan interrupted. 'You're saying, but what if they did? What if they decided to put it all together? Sha-zam! *Cosa di tutti Cosa!*'

'That's about it, buddy,' Turrin said. 'That's just about it.'

'Do the feds know about this?'

'About as much as anyone else on the outside. I've been

hearing rumbles since I was elevated to underboss rank, but even at my level it's no more than an occasional remark or a slipped word here and there. Speaking of feds. Uh, I was talking to Brognola today. About you. He uh . . .'

Bolan said, 'Why you lousy fink! You conned me!'

Turrin emitted an embarrassed snort and replied, 'Okay, so I slipped on purpose. But why *don't* you look into it?'

'What can a dead man see?' Bolan asked quietly.

'Brognola feels that a guy as dead as you could see almost anything. He's still willing to go to bat for you. He thinks he can get you a federal portfolio, especially if—'

'No, dice, Leo. Tell Brognola thanks but I'll stay alive my own way. As for this *big thing*, I'll keep my eyes and ears open.'

'Okay, but keep them *wide* open. Avoid taxicabs, bars, and all public places. That's where the mob is concentrating their look. And, uh, on this other thing . . . according to my feel, the thing is really coming to a boil and the tensions are high. This is why the New York mob is so unhappy with Gambella. They feel that he waved a red flag in your face at the most sensitively inopportune time. Or that's the rumbles I get, at my level. Right now *all* of the bosses are out of your city, even Gambella – have been all day – and you know what that means.'

'A council,' Bolan said.

'Yeah, and a very touchy one. They've got a joint somewhere out on Long Island I think where—'

'Stoney Lodge,' Bolan sighed.

'Yeah. You do get around. So I'm impressed. I just heard about it myself today for the first time. Oh, and by the way – I looked into the election thing there. Nothing. So I don't know what to figure, I mean I can't read the timing.'

'How about my girls?' Bolan asked. 'You've talked about everything but them.'

'Yeah, well I guess that's because it's bad news all the way, Sarge. They've got them. Since last night sometime.'

'Okay,' Bolan said, his voice tightening. 'Where?'

'I don't know. I can poke my nose in just so many places, you know, without getting it burnt off. All I know is that they definitely have them, both of them. Check me for wrong. A delicious brunette babe with milk'n honey complexion and an unbelievable body. An older woman-of-the-world who knows where it's at and what to do with it, also a beauty.'

'That's them,' Bolan groused. 'So your *tutti fruiti* can go to hell, Leo. I've got my own war to think about first.'

'It's all the same war, Sarge,' Turrin said faintly.

Bolan sighed. 'Yeah, I guess it is.'

'Well, *di tutti*, buddy. Time's up.'

Turrin hung up, and Bolan told the dead connection, 'Yeah, time is definitely up.'

He left the phone booth, returned to the VW and he mused aloud to his reflection in the windshield, 'The time is up for me and thee, girls. Now where the hell do we go from here?'

So Bolan had mis-read and mis-gauged Freddie Gambella. So much for options. The crafty old bastard had exercised all of them at once. And why not? That old saw about a bird in the hand versus two in the bush was as valid as ever. Gambella could snatch the girls and still play soft games with Bolan.

Well – so nothing had changed, except that now Bolan knew precisely where things stood. He did not have to try outguessing Gambella on strategy, and that was a poor game anyway when the other side held all the options. So things were simpler now, from Bolan's point of combat-view. Gambella had the girls. Bolan had to get them back. It was as simple as that.

Now. How best to accomplish that simple feat? With thirty-two thousand cops on your back? Plus, at conservative estimates, close to a thousand Mafia soldiers and an indeterminate army of bought politicos, made cops, free-lance street gangs, waiters, cabdrivers, bartenders – God knew who else. Even the dogs on the streets, maybe, were . . .

Bolan's mind froze around that thought. Dogs! Stoney Lodge! Gambella had left home early in the morning. If one could believe his wife – and Bolan could, considering the circumstances – he went away saying he had a date with some girls. And all the New York bosses congregating at Stoney Lodge. Would Gambella have taken those girls out to . . . ?

No. No. Women were supposed to be *verboten* at the joint. No woman allowed at Stoney Lodge. And yet . . .

Turrin had said something about the bosses being unhappy, that Gambella was *waving a red flag at Bolan* at a most sensitive time. Well hell! *The bosses should have been overjoyed with a red flag in Bolan's face!* Especially if it was keeping him dancing around Manhattan looking for a couple of girls who meant not a damn thing to them – while they plotted their *tutti* thing in the peace and quiet of the countryside.

But . . . if crafty Freddie the Fox was exercising double options again . . . if he was throwing his weight against the other bosses and dragging a couple of girls into the sanctum of Stoney Lodge against all tradition, just to make certain he'd keep *two* birds in the hand . . . if he meant to keep Bolan off balance and chasing whippoorwills around Manhattan while the *pigeons* were securely fastened to . . .

Goddammit, it figured! Double-option Freddie, the *Capo's Capo*, the most logical guy in the world to conceive of a *Cosa di tutti Cosa*. Freddie Gambella played for *all* the marbles, *all* the time. He was a real *tutti Capo*. Yeah, by God, it figured.

Okay, Freddie.

Get ready.

You're about to meet Bolan *di tutti* Bolan.

CHAPTER SIXTEEN

MOVEMENTS

THE VW, Bolan decided, was in danger of becoming a hot vehicle. Maria Gambella had seen it; perhaps others had, also, during the recent series of strikes. So, regretfully, it was time for a change.

He returned the micro-bus to the same 'dealer' and traded it in on a Ford Econoline, a dark green job with plenty of poop beneath the hood and a good van-configuration. For an extra twenty dollars, the guy made up nicely-artistic decals for the sides, ISLAND PARCEL SERVICE.

Then Bolan invested some more precious time in a second buying trip to the William Meyer arsenal, where he unloaded quite a chunk of money for various items of intensely pure warfare. Another thirty minutes were spent in loading and arranging the purchases in the van.

Next he set up a meet in Central Park with MacArthur and Perugia, the CIG people, in whom he confided the size and complexity of his immediate goals, though not the details. They rapped briefly on the problems confronting everybody from the inroads of organized crime, and Bolan hauled out maps and conducted a light briefing in which he emphasized the 'non-combatant nature' of their participation in the coming operation. He marked up a duplicate set of maps and turned them over to MacArthur, along with an item of ordnance, then the three of them synchronized their watches and Bolan made ready to depart.

Perugia followed him to his vehicle and told Bolan, 'I'd like to go with you.'

Bolan gave him a sizing look and regretfully shook his head. 'Sorry, Steve, no deal.'

'Why the hell not?'

'Because you're a greenhorn,' the Executioner bluntly told him. 'And it's just too damn risky.'

'I'll take my chances,' the youth insisted. 'I have a right to go.'

'*What* right?'

'You're not Italian, are you?'

Bolan grinned and shook his head. 'But some of my best friends are.'

'And some of your worst enemies,' Perugia pointed out. 'That's the whole point. You have any idea how many Italian-Americans there are?'

'No I don't,' Bolan replied.

'I don't either, exactly, but there've been about six million Italian immigrants alone, over the years. That ought to tell something.' He grinned. 'If you know anything about the average size of an Italian family, it should tell a hell of a lot. We make up a big chunk of this country.'

'So?' Bolan asked, but he already knew where the kid was headed.

'So how many of us do you figure are mixed up in organized crime?'

Bolan smiled and said, 'Save your breath. Anybody with half a mind knows that the Mafia is just a fluff of scum on the Italian community, so—'

'Well then there's a lot of half-minded people running around,' Perugia told him. 'I resent hearing Mafia jokes every time my name is mentioned.'

Bolan said, 'So would I. But that's no reason to go get your head blown off by a Mafia gun. Those people might be scum, but they're damned dangerous scum. They know their business, and it's no place for a greenhorn. I'm sorry, Steve. I won't take you.'

'It's my fight,' Perugia insisted.

'Then do your thing,' Bolan suggested. 'And leave me to do mine. You do the talking, I'll do the killing. Okay?'

'That's not what I—'

'I'm sorry,' Bolan said, in a tone that left no room for rebuttal. He drove away and left the kid staring after him.

There was more than one reason why the Executioner was not taking any riders. He intended to blitz back through Manhattan on his way across, purely as a red herring tactic, and there was no room in those plans for a college kid.

And he did blitz. He knocked over a pool hall in Harlem and walked off with the day's lottery bag, then he hit a club on Manhattan's West Side which was owned by Manny Terencia, a Gambella underling, and executed two of Manny's soldiers. Next he invaded a law office on Park Avenue and terrorized the staff into producing records of payoffs to several 'made' criminal court judges.

For his fourth and final hit of the series, he walked on to a midtown construction site, sought out one Jake Carabonzo, a loanshark contact and shylocker known as *Payday Jake*, handed him a marksman's medal, and shot Payday Jake between the eyes. As Bolan withdrew through a curious gathering of burly construction workers, he heard one of the hardhats remark, 'Jake finally got his accumulated vigorish.'

A few minutes later, Bolan had a telephone conversation with the same newsman he'd talked to earlier, gave him the details of the latest hits, and promised, 'I am just getting started.'

And he was, but not in New York City. He turned his sights toward Long Island, telling his troubled eyes in the rearview mirror, 'The difference is getting narrower all the time.'

Less than thirty minutes of daylight remained when Bolan reached the hardsite. He cruised past in a casual recon and noted that the gatehouse was manned. Two hardmen leaned against the iron gate, on the inside, talking. They swivelled their heads to watch the van go past, then resumed their conversation. Also, Bolan noted, someone was inside the gatehouse itself, probably several someones.

He went on beyond the property and pulled on to a high rise of ground for a binocular survey of that side, then circled back along a series of interconnected dirt roads to reach the observation point of his earlier visit.

Then he settled into a quiet surveillance. No dogs down there, he noted, but plenty of people. Bolan surmised that the dogs had been used for routine security, at times when the joint was not in use. Those dogs had been trained to attack any and all except their handler, that much had been patently obvious. So they would not be allowed to patrol when visitors were afoot. Bolan liked that idea, and he wondered also how the handler had rationalized the disappearance of the two which Bolan had dragged away. The continuing snowfall would have erased all signs within a very short while – so how would the guy account for the missing dogs? He smiled over that thought and continued his binocular scan in the waning daylight.

A number of vehicles were in the parking area. Lights beginning to come on here and there within the lodge. Men idly patrolling the grounds on foot, trampling down the snow – with Thompsons draped across their chests – Bolan counted six, appearing cold and disgruntled. He wondered how long they'd been out there and how often they were relieved. Those things mattered. Alertness and vigor were important attributes for a defending force. The defense was required to sweat through the monotonous routine, unable to key up and stay tight when no clear threat was visible, forced to contend with personal discomfort – and the more tired and bored they became, the more they questioned the necessity for all this hardship.

Yet, those things mattered. In a game such as this, most of

the options were with the *offense*, and Bolan meant to make full use of everything he could get going.

So he watched the patrols, continued a scan of the windows at the main lodge and those of the smaller buildings, and he began putting together a composite idea of the total scene down there.

In a large room off the ground floor veranda, a conference was in progress. Twelve to fifteen persons were inside that conference room. He arrived at this figure by counting the traffic in dinner trays which were being carried in, and the dirty glasses leaving, plus noting various seemingly insignificant details such as the number of bodyguards lurking about in the adjacent room, the number of 'waiters' streaming in and out, the activity in the kitchen, and the lineup of waiting silver buckets with wine bottles chilling in ice.

So ... twelve to fifteen ... and only five New York bosses. Turrin had made no mention of other members of *La Commissione* trekking in. So who, besides the bosses, was there? Not underbosses, Turrin had made that quite clear – this stuff was strictly top level.

Going on the number of vehicles in the parking area, with other observations, Bolan decided that fifty to sixty men were inside that compound. So ... thirty-five to forty-five hardmen ... and probably the cream of the town.

Lights were beginning to come on in the three smaller buildings clustered about the lodge. The lights for the grounds and on the wall were also on – ready for the night.

One of those small buildings was an armory. Bolan could see the gunracks through the windows along with sporting gear, targets, and so forth.

Another seemed to be a sort of lounge area for the troops. He could see the corner of a pool table, a small bar, several men sitting around in leather chairs drinking beer from cans and talking, a few metal bunks. Sure, a bunkhouse, and about ten guys on R and R.

In the final fading light of the day, bolstered by a sudden lamp flaring on from within, Bolan saw a woman move across a window of the third building. He froze, and sharpened the field of the binoculars and waited, and he saw her again, moving past in the background, hardly more than a shadow, but definitely the shadow of a woman with a rather familiar movement – even glimpsed so fleetingly – a sort of gliding feline movement.

Bolan smiled, and sent up a silent thanks to Rachel Silver's special angel, and he watched that house with an intense interest and took note of significant things, and began to mentally fill in the outline for his own movements in the coming night.

Sure, it figured. Not even Freddie Gambella had the heft to bring skirts into that sanctorum. On to the grounds, maybe, into an outhouse, maybe – but not through those consecrated doors of *Our Thing*.

Some time after the shades of darkness had draped completely about Stoney Lodge in a mantle of foreboding, Bolan looked at his watch and withdrew to the van to begin his countdown into the purest movement of warfare *The Executioner* had ever undertaken.

This one was for all the marbles. *Tutti o niente*, Freddie, *all or nothing*. And the winner take all.

CHAPTER SEVENTEEN

TIMING

BOLAN was wearing an ordinary business suit, of the type usually affected by Mafia soldiers, a bulky gray topcoat with the collar pulled up – light blue shirt with a wide flashy tie, and a snapbrim hat pulled on square and low on the eyebrows. Beneath all that he wore the shoulder harness with the silent Beretta, a short stiletto with a needle-sharp point, and a .38 revolver was thrust casually into the waistband of his trousers. He carried a bulky canvas bag over one shoulder and he was humming an Italian wedding song as he walked casually across the grounds towards the big building.

One of the patrols, about ten feet off Bolan's path, raised a hand casually and said, 'Ay.'

'Ay,' Bolan said back to him. 'Jesus I'm too cold to fart.'

'Me too,' the patrol growled.

'Well, try to relax,' Bolan called over his shoulder. 'This can't last much longer.'

'God I hope not.'

Bolan heard another voice in the darkness call over, 'Hey, what'd he say?'

'Said it won't last much longer,' the first guy replied.

'If those guys had to palavar out *here*,' complained the invisible speaker, 'it'd been over ten hours ago.'

'You ain't shittin',' said his companion in suffering.

Bolan grinned to himself and went on to the back door of the main building. A soldier in an overcoat was standing just inside the kitchen with his back resting against the glass panel of the door. Bolan pushed on the door and the guy moved away.

Speaking from outside, Bolan growled, 'Hey what the hell are you doing in there?'

'Warmin' my toes,' the guy replied defensively. 'Hell I thought I'd lost 'em.'

'Well, you better get some coffee to these boys out here. Their turds are freezing inside of them.'

'Yeah, sure,' the guy said.

'And put something stiff in it.'

'I thought the boss said no—'

'Bullshit what th' boss said. These boys are turnin' into statues.'

'Okay,' the guy said, the surly face breaking into a wide grin.

'Get 'em something to chew on, too.'

'Christ they just had supper an hour ago.'

'I don't give a shit if they had it ten minutes ago,' Bolan snapped. 'Get 'em something to chew on.'

'Well like what?'

Bolan snorted disgustedly and replied, 'Like anything. Jesus do you have to have somebody hold your dick when you pee?'

The guy moved away muttering to himself. Bolan closed the door and went on to the corner of the building, smiling over his private joke. Laced coffee and Italian pastries would get the outside men pretty well relaxed and diverted, he guessed. He stepped into the shadows at the rear for a close inspection of the main power box, a facility which he had noted during his recon of the previous night.

He set the canvas bag on the ground and removed a glob of plastic explosive, carefully molded it around the cable where it entered the box, inserted a detonator-timer, and went on.

Bolan circled the house, muttering a greeting to a sentry on the porch in front. 'Ay, stay alert there,' he told the guy.

The sentry eased up from a chair and stretched his back. 'Let's all go to Miami for the winter,' he suggested humorously.

Bolan kept to the shadows and replied, 'Freddie catches you sittin' down on the job, you might go to Miami for permanent.'

'Maybe you have to worry about Freddie,' the guy said. 'That's your problem. Augie ain't that stiff.'

The reference was to Augie Marinello, until very recently regarded as the strongest boss in New York. Bolan tried his luck and told the sentry, 'You better worry about Freddie until this meet is over. He's the man with the say.'

The sentry coughed, and walked to the edge of the porch to spit. Then he told Bolan, 'Yeah, I guess you're right.'

The Executioner suggested, 'Go on back to the kitchen. I got what's-his-name gettin' up some stiff coffee and snacks for you outside boys. Go on, you better get yours before he forgets you're out here.'

The guy was trying to get a clear look into Bolan's face. Between the upturned coat collar and the brim of the hat, there was little more than a pair of eyes. That curious code of Mafia ethics prevented the common soldier from asking the simplest of all questions. He merely nodded and asked Bolan, 'You covering for me here?'

Bolan said, 'O' course. But don't be too long.'

'Okay.' The guy hurried down the steps and disappeared around the corner of the building.

Bolan went on up to the porch, opened the screen doors, and inspected the massive double doors that guarded the sanctorum. They were made to swing together, like the doors of an old-fashioned vault, and the locking mechanism was as good. The hinges at either side would have held a Cadillac together. Bolan went to work with his plastics, wedging in a thin trail along the hinges and around the entire jamb area. A little bit of this stuff, he realized, went a hell of a long ways. He completed the job and went on, leaving the sentry post 'uncovered'. Let the wise guy worry about it, he thought.

He crossed to the armory building, looked in through the windows, saw nothing moving in there, and stepped inside. There were cases upon cases of ammo, of all sizes and types, and racks of hand weapons of every description. All was under lock and key, and Bolan meant to keep it that way. Again he made plastic molds, placed them liberally, and got out of there.

Three patrolmen were standing in a little clutch behind the building, quietly talking and relaxing over coffee and pastries. Bolan went over to them, maneuvered his back to the nearest light and said, 'I see you got the stuff.'

'Oh *you're* the guy,' someone said. 'You're a real gentleman. I gotta say that. I was startin' to think nobody knew we were here.'

'Don't you worry,' the Executioner replied. 'Somebody knows.'

'Ay, this coffee hits the spot,' another one remarked.

Bolan laughed and said, 'And that's exactly the spot you want to hit, right?'

The three patrolmen guffawed appreciatively and a tall skinny one remarked, 'There's another spot I wouldn't mind hitting. Have you *seen* those broads Freddie brought out here?'

Bolan chuckled and said. 'Mustn't touch, boys.'

'Yeah that's Freddie's private reserve,' another commented. He gave a dirty laugh and added, 'He's savin' them for a special party with Mack the Bastard.'

'Ay, have you heard the latest about that nervy shit?' the skinny one piped up. 'Tony got it on his transistor a while ago, that cocksucker is tearin' up Manhattan again. He got Payday Jake and some of Manny's boys, I hear.'

'I hear he knocked over Paoli's Poolhall,' another remarked in a subdued voice.

'I guess I just as soon be out here, freezin' my ass off,' a guy murmured.

'Freddie oughta give 'm back those broads,' the skinny one said. He winked and added, 'Slightly used, o' course.'

Bolan laughed. 'O' course. Well that's what I came out for.' He laughed again. 'No, not to slightly use 'em, but I wouldn't mind that neither. I just got to look in on 'em.'

'Ay, tell Freddie we're keeping good eyes on 'em.'

Bolan chuckled and went on to the front of *the* house. Curtain were drawn across the windows but he could see all there was to see. It was a single large room with a small toilet visible through an open door to the rear, a couch, several chairs, card tables, the usual provisions for common soldiers.

Paula was lying on the couch, a forearm draped across her face, the ripe bosom staggering somewhat as though she were having herself a quiet cry. The muscles bunched in Bolan's jaw and he stepped to the other window for a better view of Rachel. She was wearing slacks and a clinging blouse and she was seated on the floor, facing a corner in a Lotus position, unmoving, to all appearances undisturbed and unharmed. Both girls looked okay. He sighed and went on, passing back by the clustered patrol and tossing them a wave as he passed.

Another pair were standing together near the rear corner of the main lodge, enjoying their alcoholic coffee. Bolan told them, 'Dont be too long. And, hey, don't be so obvious. Why don't you step around to the back until you finish that stuff.'

What the hell, if the mob didn't have sense enough to have a Corporal of the Guard, Bolan was only too happy to play the role.

The sentries said nothing but slowly drifted around the corner out of sight. The Executioner stepped immediately on to the veranda and went softly to the line of windows at the big conference room. The drapes were drawn and the faintest light was filtering through. He could hear the murmuring rise and fall of voices and occasionally a word or two

145

would come through clearly, but this was not his chief interest. He stood there in the darkness and laid in enough plastic to blow off the side of the building.

The clear tones of someone, a rather polished voice coming obviously from just the other side of that glass, said something about, '... must be handled with all sensitivity. You gentlemen understand that.'

Bolan nodded his head. All Mafia business was handled with 'all sensitivity.' And so was Bolan's. He set in the detonators and quietly withdrew, then casually joined the three hardmen at the rear of *the* house.

Two minutes to go. Two minutes. He had to fight to keep his eyes away from his watch, and he told the group, 'You boys better kinda hurry that up.'

'Still some in th' thermos,' the skinny one said, grinning.

'I'm just startin' to feel my toes again,' another commented. 'Thus sure was nice of you to think of this, uh, uh . . .'

Bolan swore to himself and said, 'Frankie.'

'Oh yeah. Well listen, Frankie, if Freddie treats all of his boys this way, I think I wouldn't mind making a transfer.'

'He don't,' the skinny one said. He was giving Bolan the odd look, trying to pierce the anonymity of the night. 'And I don't think I know Frankie.'

Too long, Bolan was thinking. He should have fused it closer. A guy could get away with this sort of masquerade for just so long, and then blooey buddy, the game is over.

The other hardman was saying, 'Well if I was you I'd say make friends damn quick.' He swiped at his nose and added, 'This Frankie is a gentleman.'

Bolan chuckled and said, 'You might not say that if you was in my crew.'

'I think I—'

The skinny soldier cut in with, 'What crew is that, Frankie? What territory?'

There it was, the unforgivable breach of etiquette. 'If you

have to ask,' Bolan replied a bit stiffly, 'then you better not.'

The guy shrugged his shoulders, a real dumb-ass soldier, and said, 'I just thought I knew all th' lieutenants.'

Bolan growled, 'Who th' hell said I was a lieutenant?'

The skinny one smiled nervously and replied, 'Oh well, I mean . . .'

They stood there in a strained silence.

Bolan glanced at his watch. Okay, it was okay. He growled, 'Finish the coffee and get back on your posts.'

The third man, who had said very little, took a deep breath and declared, 'Well that sure hit the spot. Thanks, Frankie. You know we all appreciate it.'

And then it came . . . a small explosion, not much more than a shotgun blast, rippling through the night. Something flashed near the rear of the main lodge. Immediately darkness descended as all lighting, inside and out, was abruptly extinguished.

The men around Bolan sucked in their breaths. A cup fell to the ground. Bolan growled, 'Heyyy.'

'What the hell?' the piping voice of the skinny one declared.

'Power box must've shorted out,' Bolan said calmly.

Just then a real rumbler came from the front porch of the lodge, lighting up the yard momentarily with a blinding flash, the harsh thunder ripping across to them behind the flash – and before that one was fully felt the real shocker came, the entire side of the lodge seemed to tear away in a shattering explosion that sent shock waves along the ground beneath Bolan's feet and battered the air about his ears.

'It's a hit!' he cried. 'Get on down there!'

'We're supposed to be watching the—'

'*Fuck* that! Get on down there and cover the bosses! I'll watch this end. Go on, move, *move*!'

The three moved, silhouetted against the rumbling flames of the lodge, their Thompsons at the ready and all three running full gallop for the scene of the explosion. Others could be heard racing about in the darkness and yelling, inside the lodge and out, and men were spilling out of the bunkhouse, off to Bolan's left.

He was yelling, 'All you soldiers down to the joint! Get a shield up down there, goddammit, and get th' bosses outta there! Goddammit, *move, move*!'

Hardmen were moving everywhere, fleeting shadows in the flame-leapt darkness, cursing and yelling, and someone started screaming, 'Water! Get some water over here!'

And Bolan was fading back into the blackness around *the* house, and kicking the door in, and he could see the anxious faces peering at him in the faintly flickering glow of the fires. He grabbed one with each hand and pulled them outside. They fought him momentarily, both of them, pounding at his face and chest with the free hand, until he spoke.

'Hey, hey, this is not time for body therapy. We have to blow this joint.'

Paula heaved a shuddering sigh and moaned, 'Thank God, oh thank God.'

And Rachel, sobbing happily and very much of this world, told him, 'I knew you'd come. I just knew it.'

CHAPTER EIGHTEEN

NIENTE

BOLAN steered the girls quickly and quietly toward the wall, then halted about twenty-five yards out and pulled them to the frigid ground. Pandemonium was reaching new heights behind them as men ran shrieking about in thunderous confusion in all directions around the furiously burning building. Bolan checked his watch and murmured, 'Just a few seconds now, just—'

And then two more explosions rent the night and compounded the pyramiding confusion. The section of wall just ahead lifted and crumbled, leaving an opening large enough to drive a truck through, while back in the other direction the Stoney Lodge arsenal went up in a towering fireball, and secondary explosions from its stores were providing an impressive monologue of their own as Bolan and his charges ran out of the rapidly lightening scene, through the break in the wall and on into the blessed darkness ahead.

He escorted them as far as the van, then told them, 'Stay on the road and keep going double-time, and don't look back. A couple of friends are waiting for you at the crossroads.'

'You're not coming?' Paula cried.

'Not just yet. I'm rear-guarding. Go on, get!'

They got, Rachel throwing him a last moist look with humble eyes, Paula smiling bravely and tossing her head into the take-off. Bolan watched them disappear, then he climbed into the vehicle and made a lights-out approach to the break in the wall, where he parked and set up shop.

He opened the side doors, flung off the overcoat and draped a heavy .45 caliber chopper around his neck, then began hastily lugging stuff to the debris piled about the broken wall.

Things down in the compound were getting more frantic, if anything, but he could make out a small group running toward his position. Then two more appeared out of the darkness to his right, charging down along the outside of the wall. He whirled into the challenge and flung both men back with a short burst from the chopper, then spun around to check the progress of the group approaching from the interior.

That group were about halfway between the lodge and the wall, beautifully outlined in the backdrop of leaping flames. Bolan selected his weapon, waited, then raised a grenade launcher to his shoulder, sighted along the short range, and let fly – corrected, flew again, then again, and the walking line of explosions hurled bodies off at weird angles to the line of advance, and the advance faltered and halted, and some guy down there was groaning, calling for help, and the entire group withdrew with their wounded.

Bolan let them go. He was busy with other things. He was performing the clumsy task of being both loader and gunner for a long, shoulder-fired rocket launcher known as *bazooka*. And down there in the pandemonium he noted a cluster of men running into the building where Paula and Rachel had been kept; he carefully sighted it in, then punched off, and the armor-piercing missile whooshed off, closing the range with a shattering impact. The building lurched and puffed. Bolan saw no one running back out of there; already he was reloading and pivoting on his knee to line up on the big flaming mess of Stoney Lodge.

Again, and again the ornery rockets whizzed down the range, the old structure huffed and puffed and began falling apart faster than it could burn, and the men stopped running around down there and began thinking seriously about some way to remain alive.

Bolan knew that they were beginning to get their heads back where they belonged. A heavy returning fire from automatic weapons was feeling for his position, and he was wishing that it was time to begin vacating.

He glanced at his watch and put the bazooka aside in favour of the grenade launcher. Foot soldiers were coming again. He began laying in his pattern, carefully watching his flanks, every few seconds casting a glance toward the sky over the crossroads where MacArthur and Perugia were waiting for the girls.

Finally it came, the pyrotechnic display that told Bolan, 'A-OK, man, we got 'em,' and not until then did Bolan heave a sigh of relief and begin his cautious withdrawal.

He stowed his weapons in the van, cast another glance skyward at the final settling cinders of the signal flare, and made a quiet run toward the next firing line.

Freddie Gambella was staggering around outside in his shirtsleeves with not even any damn shoes on wondering *Christ* what had happened! Talk about 1-2-3, if that rotten shit was behind all this – well of course he was behind it – it didn't take no mental giant to figure that out! First that little popping sound and all the damn lights going off, then before Freddie could even adjust his eyes to the dark, *wham,* there goes the goddam front of the house and the whole damn place is already shaking, and then wh-wh-*wham,* the biggee, the whole goddam side of the house falls in and Freddie is laying over in a corner someplace, practically standing on his head, and the goddam joint is on fire, and he thinks his arm is broke, yeah, sure as hell it's broke, and *Christ* how did that sonuvabitch pull that off Freddie wanted to know!

Somebody, he didn't even know who, was helping him outside, and Freddie was yelling *the senator, the senator, save the fuckin' senator, you asshole!*

The guy is telling him, *forget the senator, forget 'im, that made son of a bitch is blowed to hell, clean to hell,* and

Freddie realizes then that this is Augie Marinello saying this.

And Augie has this blood all over his face, it looks like maybe his head is a little bit broke open, but he's walking around and tellin' the boys what to do. Some guy is yelling for water, and that would be like pissing on hell, that would almost be funny, the joint is a long ways beyond any water now.

Freddie hears his own voice yelling to forget the water, forget it, get those men out of there, get those goddamn blessed *made men* out of there, for God's sake two years work is laying in there, *get those men out of there*!

And this guy, this lieutenant by the way of Augie Marinello, is giving him this wild eye and telling him that there ain't nothing left to get out of there – no bosses, nobody, *no made men*, not nobody – and God knew Freddie and Augie had guardian angels sitting on their shoulders 'cause they were the only ones to get out.

And there's Augie, staggering around in his own blood, yelling at his boys to get it together. It's like a nightmare, a crying screaming wall-climbing nightmare. That joint, that beautiful goddam joint, that fuckin' impregnable beautiful hardsite joint is gone to hell and everybody with it, *all those million dollar made men*!

And that wasn't all, Freddie soon learned. More explosions, Christ the goddamn wall, *Christ the goddamn powder house*! Ka-boom and another ka-boom and lookit that shit fly!

Where was the sonuvabitch doing it from? And what with?

Yeah, Freddie Gambella was staggering around out there in the cold in his shirtsleeves and not even any damn shoes on, watching his world collapse around him.

'Them fuckin' broads!' he heard himself screeching. 'You run and get them fuckin' broads and drag their asses over here. I'm gonna stand out in the open where he can see me, and I'm going to stick my cock down their throats and choke 'em to death like that – we'll see what mister smart-ass thinks about that!'

Someone was saying, 'Ay, Mr. Gambella, take it easy, you're in bad shape, here you better sit down.'

And someone else was saying, 'Mr. Gambella, he already sprung the broads. I guess that's the first thing he done.'

Again he was screeching, 'Bullshit, don't tell me no sprung d'broads. You take some boys over there and bring 'em to me!'

The guys were giving each other knowing looks, then one of them shrugs his shoulders and says something dumb, something like, 'That was Frankie, I know damn well that was Frankie all the time.' He jogs off towards the little house, and some other boys trot off after him.

Then he hears Augie telling one of his lieutenants, 'Get some boys over there and see what that hole was blasted for. And you better send some over the wall up here and let them check it out from the other side. Come on, trot, I think this guy has brought a crew or two with him this time.'

Bullshit, who cared, *the goddam fuckin' made men were dead*! Two years of sweat and tears gone up in flames, and Freddie is trying to get this across to Augie, but Augie is just standing there and saying I know, I know, but how about Rocco and Philip and Johnny Satin, your brother bosses, aren't you feeling just a little sad about them too?

It still didn't seem real, it just couldn't be happening, and some guy is kneeling there over him and tying a rag around his arm – a broke arm ought to hurt more than this, shouldn't it? – then there comes gunfire, that just couldn't be possible, no gunfire until now? A chopper, a deep growler – Freddie knew that somebody was getting cut up ... then more explosions and ... *Christ* what was that?

'*What was that? Answer me, you asshole, what was that?*'

'This guy is hitting us with something I don't know what, Mr. Gambella. It's like guided missiles or something, I don't know. You just be still now and don't try to move around none.'

And Augie's worried voice, 'Rick, you gotta go get that guy. He's not through yet.'

'Geez, it's suicide, Mr. Marinello. I mean, this is like battlefield type fighting, not street fighting. This guy has got hisself an *army* out there.'

'Then you got to go against that army, Rick. We can't just sit here and take this. Get some boys and rush that hole, and do it now.'

'*I want them broads! I want them broads brought here! You hear me?*'

'You just better shut up about those goddamn fucking broads, Freddie. Or I'm liable to stick *my* dick down *your* throat!'

Where did Augie get off talking to Freddie the First that way? Where the hell did he get off saying he was gonna . . .? 'Did you say they're gone, Augie. He sprung the broads?'

Marinello's face was no more than a shimmering blob above his and it was patiently telling him, 'Now look, Freddie, you're hurt bad. You're gonna lose that arm, it's almost blown clear off. Now shut up and be still or you'll be losing more than an arm.'

Lose an arm? Freddie Gambella lose an arm? Whoever heard of a one-armed royal highness? I gotta tell you this, your royal highness, your goddamn fuckin' arm is missing.

Freddie began to laugh. *Christ* these fuckin' crazy nightmares. Hey Sam this is Fred. Wake me up, I'm having one of those goddam nightmares again. You put it down, Sammy boy, you put it down on the streets for me and thee.

And he thought he heard his old buddy Sam telling him, 'Sure, Freddie, that's me. No greater love is there but a guy will put it down for his friend.'

Put it down, Sammy. Christ, Dear God, Reverend Holy Mother, put it down for old Freddie, eh? *Wake me up outta this goddamn fuckin' nightmare, eh?*

CHAPTER NINETEEN

ANIMALS

So they had decided that it was all over, and that it was safe to abandon the sinking ship now. The vehicles were being fired up and brought around in a line on the macadam road, a caravan forming. And, behind them, Stoney Lodge now more stone than lodge, but the flames still roaring high into the sky and lighting up the entire hardsite, even the little buildings were blazing and just about all gone. Yeah, ground to powder, dust to dust, ashes to ashes.

The gates opened as the caravan approached. The procession halted there while the two gatemen scurried into waiting vehicles, then the caravan began rolling again. Ten cars, Bolan counted them coolly as each one swung through and on to the road, the headlamps courageously blazing forth, each of them a big sleek limousine that gleamed even in the darkness. And what a terrible darkness.

The Executioner checked his supply of armor-piercing rockets, recalculated the range for the bazooka , and decided that he was satisfied and ready.

He was lying in wait for them atop a knoll barely a quarter-mile from the walls of the remains of Stoney Lodge, a few hundred feet above the roadway where it jogged through a shallow valley, and he urged them, 'Come on, boys, close it up, take up that slack.'

He wanted them bunched – bumper to bumper would be ideal – but he wouldn't be greedy, he would settle for just having them all in the valley at once.

Then they were there, strung out like a railroad train

below him, taking it slow and easy on the snowpacked road, and he was sighting down on the lead vehicle.

Whoosh, one away. The missile streaked unerringly down the course, impacted on the forward doorpost, and the gleaming limousine instantly became a twisted mess of flames, stopped dead and skewed across the road in a perfect plug.

Whoosh, two away, and the rear vehicle went to hell in a hurry and all the others were squealing brakes – spinning all over the place like a crazy-quilt derailment of rail cars.

Three away, and four away, and why weren't they shooting back? – the Executioner wished that frozen lump would move out of his chest. Guys were running around down there and yelling, car doors all standing open, those that were left, guys leaping into snowdrifts trying to run up the other hill falling all over themselves and tumbling and sliding back down.

Yeah, Leo, this is what I'm accomplishing. Dead as I am, this is my accomplishment.

And five, six and seven away, *whoosh whoosh whoosh* as rapidly as the tall man with the grim face could fight another rocket into the tube and line-up again. Yeah, the scene below was an item of pure warfare. Burning and twisted and junked metal, raging flames and billowing smoke and the screams of the dying. Die, limousine, you who serve the darkness of the animal in the minds of men – die, you lousy . . .

Yes, he was killing *cars*, not men. *Cars*, the product of men's minds and hands and hearts and souls, and it was just a symbol, yeah, just a symbol of things that make me rotten. *Die*, symbols in burning twisted metal, giving way to the whoosh of another kind of technology – the exploding insanity of pure war and man's hatred for man.

And yeah, German Shepherd, you're a purer kind of animal than me, you kill because that's all you know *how* to do, and I kill because right now that's all I *want* to do.

156

God in heaven knew better! This was not what he *wished* to do, but whoosh whoosh whoosh it was a pure assault, no misses – ten of ten – and probably most of the people down there had managed to get out in time, except for those first two targets.

So good enough.

Bolan stood up, felt of the jerking muscles of his face, and he left the bazooka lying there, and he said, 'That's what I think of your *blessed thing*, Freddie.'

Then he withdrew, and got into his Ford war machine, and he shook the dust of that place from his feet.

For a little while, at least, the nightmare was over.

CREATED: THE DESTROYER
BY RICHARD SAPIR AND WARREN MURPHY

Convicted and condemned to death for a crime he didn't commit, Remo Williams has been resurrected and programmed – not as a normal, functioning human being, but as a cold, calculating death machine . . . created to destroy in order to preserve . . . a lethal weapon that has no loyalties, that can only be used in an extreme emergency . . . and aimed with the utmost care.

THE DESTROYER
0 552 09404 8   30p

THE DESTROYER: DEATH CHECK
BY RICHARD SAPIR AND WARREN MURPHY

The Brewster Forum – a collection of the world's top scientists involved in super-cerebral research projects. One of their more interesting secret studies is the drafting of a plan to control the world. A federal security agent is murdered and unless the murderer can be found and destroyed soon, the Brewster Forum may have to be eliminated along with its vital secrets. Only one force could handle the assignment – CURE, and its unique human weapon – Remo Williams . . .

THE DESTROYER
0 552 09405 6   30p